Submissive on the Run

A 1Night Stand Story

By
Tara Quan

Copyright © 2016 by Tara Quan
ISBN: 978-1-68361-083-0
Cover art by Fiona Jayde

Published by
Decadent Publishing Company, LLC

Look for us online at:
www.decadentpublishing.com

~A Note from the Author~

Thank you for picking up *Submissive on the Run*. I've always been a huge fan of Cherise Sinclair and Kresley Cole. After losing myself for countless hours amidst their sexy Dominants and feisty submissives, I couldn't resist creating my own adventurous pairs. Regardless of genre, I keep my stories lighthearted, the angst to a minimum, and the sex hot enough to make your face warm. In all my romances, I aim for a few laughs, a handful of clever twists, and a scorching happily ever after.

The Carnivore Club welcomes all fans of BDSM romance. After penning my first contribution to this series, I received several hints to center a story around the kickass dungeon monitor from *Submissive on Display*. Unable to resist, I pitched Kim against Joss Bradlee—an abrasive lawyer with a habit of saying whatever he thinks. It turns out the two have a long and complicated history, and Madame Eve has one night to put their relationship to rights.

If a sprinkling of humor and some creative interrogation techniques are your cup of tea, I hope you'll give this romantic comedy a shot. If you stumble upon some side characters you think deserve stories of their own, drop me a line at taraquan@outlook.com, or connect with me on

Facebook and Twitter. Obviously, I'm very responsive to reader requests.

Tara Quan

P.S. Interested in more spanking fun? Join my mailing list at www.taraquan.com/newsletter and get another naughty read delivered straight to your inbox.

Dedication

To the readers and editors who've commented on Kim's awesomeness, thus inspiring me to give my kickass dungeon monitor her own story.

Chapter One

Wchen rays of sunshine sneaked through the holes in her makeshift drapes, Kim Tran declared defeat. The more she chased sleep, the more it eluded her. Already losing the battle with the desert's morning heat, her underpowered air-conditioning unit emitted a low whine punctuated by intermittent creaks. As she rolled onto her back and kicked the wrinkled bed sheets off her calves, she attempted to snap out of the unending doldrums.

Wallowing in self-pity served nobody. Smile long enough, pretend hard enough, and happiness becomes reality. Until a year ago, her family's generations-old secret to a lifetime of contentment had never failed her.

But painting a false face and pursuing the illusion of optimism proved more difficult with each night she spent alone. She missed Boston, despite its blizzards and blistering winters. This month would have brought the end of spring, heralding a summer muted by cool river breezes and the occasional chill. New England's temperamental climate couldn't be more different from Las Vegas's never-ending heat.

A year ago, her major concern had been saving up for an apartment security deposit. With graduation on the verge of forcing her out of on-campus housing, she'd fretted about her senior thesis, crammed for exams between classes and part-time jobs, and siphoned away funds for certain extra-curricular activities. Instead of mentioning the "white boy" her parents would never approve of, she'd lied to them about her Memorial Day weekend plans, citing a school project as her reason for remaining in the city.

Karma turned out to be a bitch. One little lie, and she'd landed on the opposite side of the country almost a year later, strapped for cash and unable to contact her family, all thanks to the man in question.

If Joss hadn't planned a weekend getaway at his boss's beach house on Martha's Vineyard, she wouldn't have needed to borrow a computer. If she hadn't borrowed the computer, she wouldn't have spotted some odd-looking accounting software. Having studied to become an accountant, she hadn't been able to resist snooping.

If she hadn't snooped, she wouldn't be in witness protection—the shittiest kind, for crimes no one cared about. The kind where the US Marshals basically said, in somewhat nicer words, she was shit out of luck.

Yes, it all led back to kinky sex. Okay, maybe curiosity and hacking proclivities had something to do with it, but she preferred to blame hormones. She should have listened to her mother and saved sex for after she'd earned a degree. Heck, considering her current predicament, she should have waited until after she'd earned a PhD in mathematics.

To add insult to injury, one particular face persisted at haunting her waking dreams. She couldn't talk to a Dom without making an immediate comparison to her former lover, couldn't witness a scene without recalling the ones they'd shared. Since she worked as a dungeon monitor in Sin City's swankiest BDSM establishment, she'd spent most of her nights reliving the past, which came with a problematic side effect.

After close to a year of celibacy, horny didn't come close to describing her current state. Alone in bed, her thoughts detoured to sexual fantasies with frustrating regularity. If she hoped to sleep a wink before her next shift, she had to take the edge off.

Squeezing her eyes shut, she sifted through countless images of male celebrities, recent and classic, hoping one would stick. She wanted to imagine a different face, a different man, a different Dom. But her mind skipped Jamie Dornan and Chris Hemsworth, dismissed the *Star Wars* version of Harrison Ford and Brad Pitt à la vampire.

As always, her fantasy stalled on a too-familiar face, one with hard angles, an aristocratic mien, and a crooked smile equal parts vulnerable and wicked. Though she clamped her teeth on her lower lip before his name escaped, it was his pale tresses she envisioned lacing through her fingers, his jade eyes commanding her submission as a wall of muscle pinned her to the mattress. She turned her head to the side, relishing the scrape of his five o'clock shadow along her cheeks. When his tongue drew a scalding pattern down the column of her neck, she lifted her chin.

With a moan, she slid her hand inside her

dampening panties, searching and stroking, all the while pretending those fingers were his. She imagined him gripping her hips, his hard body scalding her naked flesh. Groaning, she clutched the sheets beneath her with her free hand. Her feet flattened against the rough fabric.

As she spread her labia, she could almost sense him bearing down on her, his entry crushing and unrelenting. Her thighs parted, drew back as if he'd forced them down. When she circled her clit, her inner muscles clenched around emptiness.

Edgy need built and doubled. Her harsh breaths echoed in the small room. She writhed until her T-shirt bunched up around her breasts, probed until moisture coated the juncture at the apex of her legs.

With each breath, she drew in the tart scent of sweat and frustrated desire. But no matter how hard she sought release, it escaped her. She squeezed her lids tighter, willing the mental block to snap. She was so close—

"Meeeooooaaaw"

Jolting to a seated position with a muffled scream, she glared at the cat as he jumped onto the mattress. Rising to his haunches between her legs, Tiger swished his tail back and forth. After sniffing the air, he plunked his butt down and commenced licking his paw. The innocuous feline gesture somehow damned her as the worst sort of pervert.

"That's it. I'm never masturbating again." With the whispered vow, she fell against the lumpy pillows, wiped her fingers on her T-shirt, and righted her panties. Coated in perspiration, she struggled to regulate her breathing as claw-tipped paws padded over her abdomen.

Perched on her boobs, the overweight ball of fur forced her to stare into pale-green irises that reminded her of Joss—eyes that had compelled her, against all good sense, to take the feline off the streets. God knew she didn't need another mouth to feed.

"Don't you dare judge me." She wiped at the crusted tears above his little nose with the hem of her top. "You're squatting. Polite squatters don't intrude on the hostess's privacy."

A low rumble emanated from the creature on her chest. His front paws commenced digging into her neckline as his tongue lashed out to groom her collar. Though probably less than eighteen months old, the white tabby, British shorthair mutt weighed enough to put significant pressure on her ribs. With his mouth inches away from her nose, she caught whiffs of cat breath, which reminded her of raw chicken.

Turning to her side, she sent her companion toppling onto the rumpled sheets. From the far corner of her mattress, she spied her alarm clock's digital readout. Having ended her shift at the Carnivore Club at 4:00 a.m., she'd spent the past four hours not sleeping. She'd once considered a full six hours of slumber a minimum requirement. On the night shift and possessing a circadian rhythm too stubborn to conform to needs of the service, she managed a few short naps on the best of days.

She scowled at the cat. The little devil had wreaked havoc on her chances at a quick and easy orgasm. The cat's superb ability to detect and respond to movement left her with scant privacy in the minuscule studio apartment. It'd been an eon since she'd gotten off.

Resolving to crawl out of bed to warm up some homemade pet food—a twice-a-day chore since the feline princeling turned up his nose at any store-bought offerings—she reached over to scratch his round, whiskered cheek. Swiveling his disproportionately large head with remarkable speed, he nipped her finger. When she yanked her hand back, he ambled forward to sprawl on her hair.

Grunting, she tried to tug the long, thick tresses out from under the fur ball. He refused to budge, trapping the waist-length black strands beneath his heft and giving her one more reason to look forward to next week, when she'd scheduled her haircut and annual donation to Locks of Love. Unlike in Boston, Las Vegas' perpetual heat turned her one attempt at charity into a 24-hour torture device.

She batted at the cat's nose with her knuckles. "Do you want to eat, or not?"

Tiger bared his teeth, whacked her hand, and yawned.

"I'm guessing no." Grabbing the spare pillow, she plopped it over her face to shield her from the intensifying sunlight and the cat's morning breath. With a thud, Tiger pounced. Through the pillow, she detected one paw on her forehead and another on her cheek. His purr rumbling like a small engine, the feline shifted his weight from one leg to the other.

Face massage, kitty-style. There must be worse ways to start the morning, but she struggled to divine a single one.

As if in answer to her mental query, her cell phone trilled. With a whimper, she groped blindly along the left side of her mattress. Finding nothing, she extended her arm toward the floor, scooting it around until the side of her hand hit a vibrating hunk of metal. A shorter dropping distance for electronic devices numbered among the few perks of not owning a bed frame.

She tapped her thumb on random locations at the bottom half of the screen until the ringing stopped. Shoving the phone under her pillow, in the general vicinity of her face, she grumbled, "Hello?"

"I woke you up, didn't I?"

Bolting upright, she sent the cat tumbling down her chest and onto her lap. Ignoring Tiger's claws as he scrambled up her boobs to perch on her shoulder, she held the phone against her ear with one hand and used the other to grab the baseball bat she'd positioned next to the mattress.

When she vaulted to her feet, the far-from-nimble feline toppled off, leaving behind burning streaks as he attempted to slow his descent by digging his claws into her shirt. She stared past the kitchen area and focused on the door. Located in the basement of a four-story walkup, her place had a single entry point. For a long moment, she waited for something to happen, the silence absolute but for steady crackles as breaths hit the microphone on the other end of the connection.

"How did you get my number?" No need to confirm the caller's identity. Nothing could erase his voice from her memory vault.

"The usual way—I hired someone. I have to say, the US government sucks at hiding people. Talk about a lazy ass name change. They added all of three letters—l, y, and g."

Given their general ambivalence, she'd been surprised they'd bothered to do anything beyond patting her shoulder and advising her to "stay safe." Her borrowed identity came courtesy of a distant cousin, Kimber*ly* Tran*g*, who had gone on a prolonged walkabout to Australia. With no plans to return stateside, she'd agreed to exchange her driver's license and social security number for a token donation to Green Peace.

She glanced at Tiger, who had managed to circumnavigate the kitchen counter to skulk in the gap between the refrigerator and wall. Logistical issues raced through her mind. All her clean clothes were already inside a duffel, a permanent storage solution ever since circumstances forced her into a vagabond lifestyle. Getting the cat into his carrier might prove a challenge, one she could overcome in less than five minutes if she didn't mind decorating her arms with additional scratches.

"Damn it, Joss. Tell me how long I have to get out of here." With her fight-or-flight instincts shifting into overdrive, finding out how he'd tracked down her number fell off her priorities list. If he'd risked calling her after ten months of radio silence, then his family's hired guns couldn't be too far behind.

She and Tiger needed to get the hell out of Vegas.

"You don't have to go anywhere. It's over, pet. No one's coming after you."

Her heart thudded. Her ears roared. Relief and uncertainty struggled for purchase. She wanted to believe him, but life-threatening stakes prompted her to hesitate. If what he said was true, why hadn't the witness protection people contacted her? Given, the ones she'd dealt with hadn't exactly oozed competence, but informing someone their life was no longer in danger didn't strike her as a tall order.

A reasoned reaction beyond her reach, she fell back on ingrained courteousness. "I.... Thank you for letting me know."

"You don't believe me." Despite the distance and time separating them, he read her with dangerous accuracy. His incredulity grated. After everything that had happened, why would he assume she'd trust him without question?

"Of course I do." She sniffed. "Why wouldn't I?"

"Are you being sarcastic? I can't tell without facial expressions."

She massaged her nose's non-existent bridge. Picking up on social cues had never been the man's strong suit. "I'm rolling my eyes at you right now."

"Oh, don't be so skeptical. I swear to God you have your life back."

"You're an atheist."

He grunted. "Fine. I swear on my mother's grave—"

"According to yesterday's gossip rags, the wicked witch is very much alive."

"It's a figure of speech, smart ass. I *promise* she's called off the dogs. Or, well, she will in about fifteen minutes. You can come home."

"The last time I took what you said at face value...." Her fingers tightened around the baseball bat. "It turned out you lied about everything, including your name."

"You *love* exaggeration. Joss is my name—at least to anyone who matters. I don't respond to Joseph. And while I omitted a few minor details, I never *lied*. Well, okay, I told a fib or two, but it was really a case of you jumping to the wrong conclusions."

"You're blaming *me* for your fake identity?" Rage,

pure and visceral, burned away her fear. "And there was no *us*. We fucked. We scened. Because of you, I almost died. That pretty much sums up the relationship."

Tempted to swing her weapon at the few mugs and bowls she owned, she threw the bat on the floor. It hit the peeling linoleum with a loud crack, eliciting a startled yowl from Tiger. Who was she kidding? If armed men stormed through her door, the piece of wood wouldn't do her much good.

"Who's lying now?" His absolute confidence fueled her fury. "You are the closest I have to an actual girlfriend."

"And you're the epitome of the ex from hell," she shrieked. "Your *mother* sent thugs to kill me."

"And I'm telling you I've solved the problem. I will also make keeping you alive my priority for the rest of my life. You can take that promise to the bank."

Her throat dried up. Why did he have to go and say something super nice?

Her bruised heart insisted she stay angry. Her survival instincts cautioned against prolonging contact. But she believed him. She had no idea why, but she did, making her the worst kind of gullible idiot. Her head spinning from the disconcerting realization, she sank onto the mattress and hugged her knees.

He was an asshat with a psychopathic family and enough baggage to keep a therapist employed for years.

She'd give anything to see him again.

Messed up, thy name is Kim.

As her stomach tied itself into a nauseating knot, Tiger slunk closer and brushed up against her calves.

While habitually unaffectionate, the cat had a way of knowing when she needed the feline equivalent of a hug. On the brink of cutting ties with the one person who mattered most, she could use a couple dozen.

"I don't trust you," she murmured, reminding herself of what should be true but never had been. "I have no reason to trust you."

"You're angry, and you're full of shit." Yet, a hint of uncertainty tinged his gruff voice.

"We hardly know each other." For months, they had lived a lie—a fantasy woven from half-truths and impossible dreams. "Everything between us.... It was all fake."

"No, it wasn't. I'll prove it as soon as I get this situation under control."

She scratched behind the feline's ear, drawing comfort from the silky fur and rare opportunity to snuggle. "So the situation is not *actually* under control, is it?"

"As I'd said—it'll be official in the next fifteen minutes. There was a gap in my schedule, so I thought I'd give you the good news early."

She released a pent-up breath, her muscles unknotting despite her determination to cling to doubt. Wariness ebbed, but anger blazed stronger with each word they exchanged. "In that case, I very much appreciate you doing...whatever you did."

"Always so polite." He chuckled. "I miss your goody-two-shoes routine, especially when you're telling me to go fuck myself. Look, check your email— the new one you think is all stealth. There's a plane ticket in the inbox. We'll meet at Logan—"

"No, thank you."

"That wasn't a request." All of a sudden, his tone

turned full-on Dom.

Too bad. She'd sworn off her submissive side for the better part of forever. "I'm not going back. We're not meeting at the airport or anywhere else. I didn't get the chance to tell you in person, but I assumed you'd make the logical leap. Let me spell things out. We're done."

"Oh, please. You're still mad. I get it. But—"

"For the love of all that's holy," she snapped. "How full of yourself are you? No, don't answer. I already know. For the record, if somewhere in your self-absorbed, egotistical, spoiled brat brain, you think—"

"Is the name-calling necessary?"

Closing her eyes, she counted back from ten. "We're not picking up where we left off. You are assuming it, which means you're certifiably insane. You let me jump to the wrong conclusions about who you were. You kept up the lie for months. Your *boss*, who is a scheming criminal, turned out to actually be your damn *brother*. When I tried to expose him, your mother sent a bunch of goons to corner me in a dark alley. One held a gun to my head."

"Since we're walking down memory lane, might I remind you I saved you from said goons?"

"Which proves you knew they were coming." Her screech startled the cat enough he scuttled away. Having not had the opportunity to vent for close to a year, she couldn't hold back the torrent of words tumbling out of her mouth. "I appreciate the rescue. I appreciate the getaway car and money. I even appreciate you telling me the truth before you told me to disappear. It doesn't mean I plan on seeing you ever again."

"Would you please calm down? Your soprano

impression is hurting my eardrums, and—"

"Because of you, my parents never got to watch my graduation ceremony." Her cheeks, nose, and forehead burned. "I didn't even find out my final grades."

"You passed. Summa cum laude with a shit ton of other honors. What did you think happened? You went out of your way to perpetuate the Asian geek stereotype. Think about it this way. I saved your parents from having to see you in an overpriced robe and funny black hat. Mine never did, either. It's overhyped."

For a moment, she visualized closing her fingers around his thick neck. When her stomach revolted at the image, her ire quadrupled. Why couldn't she even *think* about hurting him? "Thank you for the non-apology. Since we clearly operate on different wavelengths, it's time to end this conversation."

"If you wanted to, you would have already hung up. Admit it. You miss me. I seem to have the exact same problem, which is why I called the moment I found out your number. We've spent a year trying to forget what happened, and it didn't work. Come back to Boston. I'll convince you eventually, so you might as well save us both some time."

Before she could throw her phone at the wall, she remembered the price tag on a new one. At least she'd be able to sign up for a contract. "You're pissing me off on purpose so I'll keep talking."

"And you're playing along." A testament to her impending insanity. "By the way, you brought this shit storm on yourself. You got nosy. You're too smart for your own good, and you have no sense of self-preservation. I told you not to make a statement."

"Your brother cheated tens of thousands of people out of their life savings," she gritted out. "He emptied pension funds and retirement accounts. He stole from hospitals and charities." After filling her lungs, she exhaled and managed to dial her volume back a few notches. "Not exposing him would have been unconscionable."

"And since I put him on a private jet an hour ago, he'll spend the rest of his life on a beach resort in Tunisia. Congratulations. You put your life at risk, all so he can enjoy deep tissue massages with an ocean view."

"For the record, I hate rich, scheming assholes."

"Join the club. We have unfinished business. Let's at least meet to talk things through."

"We're talking right now." And burning through her pre-paid minutes, as a matter of fact. "I'm not flying across the continent to do the exact same thing."

"Well, I'd planned on having sex while we patched things up. I figured it'd go much faster."

On the verge of destroying her phone despite the financial repercussions, she found solace in the cat's bout of high-pitched meows. Tiger's breakfast time was in an hour or so. He might as well eat. "Are you *trying* to be obnoxious? I'm hanging up. I need to feed the cat."

"You have a cat? Men with guns were hunting you down, and you got a fucking pet? Are you *insane*?"

"Don't you dare judge—"

"But it's dumb as all shit."

"Joss."

"What?"

"Fuck off."

Chapter Two

Joseph Bradlee, III had learned at a young age to avoid pissing off his mother. Sandra Bradlee had a nasty habit of throwing breakable objects at people's heads when life refused to go her way. For the most part, he, his brother, and his father had done their best to smooth out all possible inconveniences before they soured her mood. Since mistakes happened, Joseph Bradlee, II, a staid corporate attorney born from a long line of even more staid lawyers and businessmen, had stooped to staffing his Beacon Hill estate with illegal immigrants for the sole purpose of avoiding lawsuits.

His father hadn't pursued these precautionary measures out of love, or at least Joss had never detected a hint of such devotion during the scant school breaks he'd spent at home. No, placating his trophy wife had more to do with prestige, scandal avoidance, and, above all, convincing himself he hadn't made the biggest mistake of his life.

The *actual* biggest mistake of the old bastard's sorry excuse of a life had been, in his own words, the son spawned from too much Scotch and a ripped condom, aka Joss. The child in question had lived up to his parents' rock-bottom expectations by matriculating from prep school through the sheer power of charm, good looks, and bribery. After graduating from a top-tier university that happened to have a library named in his grandfather's honor, he somehow sailed through an Ivy League law program with flying colors for the sole purpose of proving his father wrong.

Too bad his old man had conked a year before Joss could throw the bar exam's somewhat surprising results at his ever-disapproving face.

He hadn't been too surprised to discover the terms of his inheritance—a trust designed to prevent any member of their dysfunctional family from squandering generations of accumulated wealth, written under the assumption they were all the worst sorts of idiots. It had taken him forever and a day to unravel the legal silo within which billions of dollars dwelled. By then, his brother had sought alternative means for financing his expensive tastes.

Having invited Sandra to his office for the sole purpose of relaying information certain to elevate her blood pressure, Joss had seen to several safety measures. He'd removed or locked up every throwable item. For once devoid of files and loose papers, his chrome desk stood naked. His secretary had secured his laptop in the safe, removed the obligatory bowl of candy from her station, and stripped all artwork from the walls.

But they'd neglected to relocate the huge stainless steel lamp lighting his desk. After all, who would expect a sixty-something, willowy blonde to heft the appliance above her head and perform a YouTube-worthy impression of the Incredible Hulk?

After dodging the life-threatening projectile by a less-than-reassuring margin, Joss raised his palms in the air. "Mother, for shit sake, keep it together." Having anticipated a scene, he'd sent his staff on an extended brunch-break prior to his guest's arrival. The jury was out on whether he'd made the right decision.

He batted away one flying crimson stiletto in time to preserve his face, but the other's trajectory managed to coincide with his temple. Biting off a curse, he wiped the trickle of blood with his sleeve and scowled when he remembered how long his tailor took to construct French-cuffed, monogramed dress shirts to his exact specifications.

Then again, he'd bulked up over the past ten months. Faced with an unexpected dry spell, he'd channeled sexual frustration into bench presses. Overdue for updated measurements and a jaunt down Savile Row, he looked forward to killing several birds with one stone.

An all-expenses-paid shopping trip to London seemed a fitting bribe for a submissive who'd spent close to a year on the run. Kim would love his townhouse in England.

But, first, he must tend to more pressing matters. When his mother's red-tipped claws dug into the back of an Italian-designed, leather chair, Joss slammed his palm on the desk. "Enough, Sandra. One more stunt, and I swear I'll close down your expense account."

The woman's pale hands clenched hard enough green veins protruded. Nonetheless, the heavy piece of furniture remained on the floor. The best way to get his mother's attention was to threaten her expense account.

"You couldn't pull it off even if you wanted to," she hissed.

To increase maneuverability, he sidestepped his desk and retrieved the merino wool jacket strewn on the floor. Shrugging it on, he ambled toward the floor-to-ceiling windows. Located on the 49th floor of Boston's iconic Prudential Tower, his office had a stunning view of the Charles River—one of the many reasons he'd chosen this location for his law firm.

"Newsflash. Your favorite son was convicted in absentia of fraud this morning, thanks to evidence I handed the DA on a freaking platter. He's on a private jet to somewhere without an extradition treaty. According to the terms of the Bradlee Trust, committing a felony cuts him off without a cent, leaving me as the sole heir to the fortune. Call your lawyers, if you want, but trust me—I'm the person signing all your checks."

"How could you do this to him?" She stomped her foot. "He's your brother."

"You two left me no choice. You made it your mission to kill an innocent woman." His mother's cocaine habit had allowed her to cultivate more than a few unsavory acquaintances. Through those acquaintances, she'd hired assassins to kill Kim before she could testify. Joss had fixed matters so she no longer needed to.

He reacted in time to catch the slap aimed at his cheek. He winced. His mother's crimson nails appeared beyond sharp. "So you sold out your brother for your *whore*?"

"As I said, you left me no fucking choice. He's

getting off easy, Mother. Hopping around extradition-free zones isn't much of a punishment. Fraud and theft have consequences. He knew what they were. I'd listed them all to his face in this very office." Joss glared at her. "What did you think would happen?"

Her eyes narrowed to slits. "If you'd chosen your family instead of the bitch, he would have walked, and we'd all be billions of dollars richer."

"When you already have billions, billions more is kind of redundant. I told you both to be patient. All I needed was time. I challenged the trust. I succeeded. But, by then, you two had already cemented your Ponzi scheme." He shrugged. "Any way you slice it, your dumbass son screwed himself. He's aware of this. He's also aware I now hold the purse strings. His comfort is at my pleasure, which is why you're going to call off your dogs." For reasons Joss had never understood, Sandra had always favored one son above the other. She'd do anything to allow him the lifestyle to which he'd become accustomed—including not committing murder.

"It's all *your* fault." Bright red blotches marred the perfection of her Botox-smoothed skin. "He was done taking scraps from a trust your father tied up tighter than a damn chastity belt. If you'd worked faster—"

"Fine, it's my fault." Accustomed to the refrain, Joss rolled his eyes. "Either way, I have you by the balls. I'm telling you to leave my girlfriend alone."

When her fingers curled into fists, he added, "As it stands, you'll both continue to receive a monthly allowance, which is equivalent to the annual salary of most people. If you manage to dig yourself into a hole, there's a fifty-fifty chance I'll bail you out. If

Kim gets so much as a scratch on her, you will never see another dime from the Bradlee Trust. Are we clear, Sandra?"

Her chest heaved, her face turned a mottled shade, but she didn't attack. Though prone to temper tantrums and poor judgment, Sandra at least hovered a few shades shy of complete insanity. "Fine. I'll leave your slut alone."

***

"I can't believe you're getting a pet."

Joss scowled at his best friend. Nathan Winthrop, a computer genius turned billionaire, had a nasty habit of jumping to the wrong conclusions. "Shut it, Nate. Do I look like the pet type to you?"

"Then why did you lug a top-of-the-line cat carrier onto Nate's plane?" Luka Petrovich, the flight's third passenger, sipped aged single malt from a crystal tumbler. The bastard had always been too snooty for beer. "Can you imagine him with a kitty?"

The aircraft's owner snorted. Having first met in kindergarten, the three knew each other a little too well. "Remember how he killed all those Tamagotchi things back in elementary school?" When virtual pets had been all the rage, Nate had studiously dismantled the handheld plastic toys, Luka had babied his needy collection of pixels to the pinnacle of health, and Joss had helped the creatures ascend to virtual heaven by watching them stew in digital piles of shit.

Nate pointed his thumb over his shoulder at the carrier sandwiched between the reclining leather seats and the aircraft's well-stocked bar. "But the man obviously thinks he's taking an animal back.

First the cars, and now this. Must be an early onset midlife crisis. It's supposed to hit in your fifties, not at the beginning of your thirties."

Joss geared up to explain, opened his mouth, and scowled when Luka cut him off.

"It's a chick crisis, not a midlife crisis. I'm sure because he traded his shoe wall to me for a favor." Setting his glass on the mahogany armrest, the conniving extortionist rubbed his palms together. "I can't wait to turn some of that mint-condition, never-been-worn footwear into doggie chew toys. I plan on recording his ugly mug while I toss the original boxes in the dumpster."

Joss's stomach churned.

Leaning forward, Nate placed his elbows on his thighs. "Get out of here. He's been collecting those sneakers since we were ten."

Eight, but who was counting? "I don't know why Luke even wanted them." Three could play the third-person references game. "He doesn't believe in shoes without stitched leather soles."

"Some of the rarer models fetch a mint on eBay, and I'm in the market for a new car." Luka erased a scuff on his glossy wingtips with the pad of his thumb. "Better yet, think of all the things I can make him do to earn those shoes back, one pair at a time. I'm pretty sure a certain someone will be willing to post wiener pics on Twitter."

Having the entire world glimpse grainy photos of his dick didn't bother Joss one bit. No point tipping his hand, however. "I'm your fucking lawyer. This past year, you've needed me to defend you in court, sue for damages, and file for a restraining order. It's a matter of time before you come begging for something else."

"You forget Luke's current sub isn't as crazy as his ex." Angling his broad frame away from Joss, Nate asked, "What favor forced Mr. Scrooge to cough up his pride and joy? It had to be huge."

"That's the thing. It wasn't. I paid for and sent an invitation. It took all of five minutes." With a jerk of his chin, Luka indicated the red envelope on the coffee table. "Since he has a matching card, I'm guessing someone is orchestrating a hot date."

Nate snagged the invite. His dark eyebrows rose as he pulled out the card. "Isn't this the escort service he hooked you up with a few weeks ago?"

"Stop calling it an escort service." Luka threw a glance over his shoulder, as if expecting his sub to materialize behind the seat. "Naomi and I are together because of it, remember? Insulting Madame Eve will get me in all kinds of trouble."

"Pussy whipped," Joss muttered under his breath. "If I'd known they'd get this serious, I would've never shelled out the dough for his stupid one-night stand."

For once, their mutual friend seemed to share his chagrin. "Yeah. If I hadn't been at the collaring ceremony, I'd have figured she's the one wielding the crop. Considering how this killjoy turned out, why the hell are you lugging the envelope around? It's a scourge on bachelorhood."

"It's also an easy way to gain access to the Carnivore Club on the down-low." And to trap a certain stubborn submissive in a sealed room. "They run a tight ship at this Vegas joint. I want my visit to be a surprise."

"You're pretty full of yourself, but isn't the cat carrier a bit much? She's not going to move to a different city with you after one date." Luka's lack of confidence grated.

"The carrier is plan B"

"Plan B?"

"While I keep her occupied, you are going to break into her apartment and steal the cat."

Nate crossed his arms. "If this works out, you're going to need couples therapy. And if you think I'll participate in cat-napping, you're delusional."

"It's not cat-napping *per se*. More like cat-borrowing. I'll threaten to take the thing with me and see if she calls my bluff. And yes, you're going to help. You owe me."

"I really fucking don't."

"Fine. If you do this, I'll owe you." From Nate's expression, the man was tempted. "You want me to owe you. You've wanted me to owe you for decades."

Luka chuckled. "We should play along. I want to find out how this ends. I'll put a hundred bucks on the woman kicking Joss's ass."

"We don't need more than one person to grab a damn cat," Nate grumbled. "Besides, aren't I paying you to do a job?"

An architect, Luka had been hired to redesign the offices of a tech startup Nate had acquired. The project entailed regular trips to Sin City. "And when I finish for the night, I'll swing by to watch a DM smack him upside the head."

"So mystery girl is a dungeon monitor. I'd always pegged his type as petite brunettes."

"Oh, it is. But I've watched this particular petite brunette literally crush a man's balls. Wouldn't mind a repeat performance."

"You do realize I have a black belt in Jujitsu," Joss

drawled. "Show me some respect, or I'll triple my retainer."

He might as well have not spoken. "We'll meet up at the club after you're done cat-napping and I'm done with work."

Nate steepled his fingers. "I don't see any other choice. Our unfortunate, potty-mouthed friend needs all the support he can get. The man's track record with women is a lifelong series of slaps in the face—at least from the ones who hadn't researched the Bradlee Trust in advance. Too bad he has some sort of radar for detecting gold-diggers."

Since Joss needed the pair around for his scene to play out, he offered a token protest. "Please. I've gotten real good at catching slaps before they hit. Don't you have something better to do?"

"Can't think of a single one." Luka loped to the bar for a Scotch refill. Good friend that he was, he returned with an uncapped Blue Moon for Joss. "While I hate messing up my sleep cycle, the prospect of watching you crash and burn is too tempting."

Accepting the beer, Joss quirked an eyebrow. "Not gonna happen. When I *really* want something, I always get it. I *really* want this runaway sub back."

***

"Didn't your shift end six hours ago?" Kim paused at the small table in the employee locker room, where the Carnivore Club's part-time bartender had set up two laptops, three tablets, and five different smartphones.

Sumona Mehta, referred to by most dungeon monitors as Moni M, so as not to be confused with

Moni B, nudged a pair of tortoiseshell reading glasses up her nose. "All I need in life is free Wi-Fi and power outlets." She reached for a giant mug emblazoned with NERD-GASM. "Oh, and a sugar delivery system."

The hot chocolate left a smear on the resident geek's white teeth, the color a shade darker than her mahogany skin. Black curly hair escaped her tight braid, puffing out to form a somewhat lopsided halo around her heart-shaped face. Her oversized T-shirt displayed the police call box from Dr. Who.

Kim pointed at the oversized duffel on the floor. "Someone's settling in. Are your parents hounding you to register for Shaadi.com again?" Quick to adapt to the digital age, the Indian subcontinent's diaspora had taken the screening process for arranged marriages online.

"Geesh. I'm twenty-three, not thirteen. I have bigger problems than Mom's daily dose of matrimonial pressure. One would think a genius IQ and PhD from Cal Tech would broadcast my lifelong goal of spinsterhood, but no. She's determined to marry me off before I hit the officially on-the-shelf mid-twenties."

After checking her watch, Kim settled on one of the vacant seats. "So, you're here because your mom staked out your apartment?"

"I wish." Moni heaved a sigh. "I'm dodging a rich white guy who won't take no for an answer."

Intriguing, especially since the woman's dating experience seemed confined to the virtual variety. "A *hot* rich white guy?"

Moni wagged a finger. "Don't go around spreading rumors. He's interested in my patents, not me."

"Your *pants*? Please, tell me more."

"No, my *patents*. When my dodgy former business partner sold his half of our startup, he neglected to mention *I* own all the intellectual property. Based on the emails and voice mails I received, the pissed-off buyer found out a few days ago."

"Okay, my interest level tanked." Kim slumped. "This story was better before it turned all geek."

Her friend laughed. "If it helps, I googled the buyer. He's hot, assuming you're into broad chests, dark hair, and big blue eyes. He's also six-foot something."

Though her type had narrowed to a very specific, equally tall, green-eyed blond, Kim made a show of fanning her face. "Who *isn't* into that? Anyway, if he's calling, I'm sure he's willing to give you big bucks for those patents. Why don't you call him back?"

With her finger, Moni drew a circle above the array of smartphones on the table. "I need them for my Kink-dar."

Kim suppressed a wince. "I still think you should come up with another name."

"Meh. I invent. Branding isn't my thing. Once it's done, I'll pitch it to some venture capitalists, and someone else can deal with trademarks. Anyway, I want to see this through. Imagine if every sub and Dom could get an alert whenever their kink-mate is nearby. Won't it make life so much easier?"

"I think there's more to compatibility than a limit list, but what do I know?" Her sex life had wallowed in the gutter for close to a year. "Anyway, my shift's starting. Have fun with your...err...coding thing."

"Wait, wait. Reception dropped this off for you." After a bit of shuffling, Moni unearthed a red envelope from under one of the tablets. "Apparently, you have an admirer."

Reading the scribbled note under the sender's address, Kim grinned. "Nah. I rescued a club member from a sticky situation with his ex a while ago. This is his way of paying me back. I hadn't expected a Dom to bother with thank you cards, but...."

Her brows snapped together as she read the text. *Madame Eve cordially invites you to a one-night stand. Please meet your date in the Carnivore Club's interrogation room at 3:00 a.m. This service cannot be exchanged, refunded, or gifted to someone else.*

"I'd already snuck a quick look," Moni confessed. "You must have done some serious ball-busting. Rumor has it Madame Eve's service is exclusive to people with money to burn."

Kim sighed. "I wish he hadn't. I'm *so* not in the place to date."

"I didn't see anything in the envelope about *dating*. Relationships are so pre-2000s. Why else would I slave away at this app? As for your plans tonight, it seems you are pre-paid for a scene with a compatible Dom. Why not go?"

Springing to her feet, Kim shook her head. "The last time I tried no-strings sex, the arrangement extended into a several-month-long limbo before blowing up in my face." She omitted the part about actual gunfire. "I'm not stupid enough to jump down that rabbit hole twice."

Moni arched her thick black eyebrows. "From the few hints you'd dropped, it seems like you attempted this arrangement with someone you knew—a friends-with-spanking-benefits sort of deal. Showing up in the interrogation room today is different. The Dom will be a complete stranger."

"I don't do stranger sex.'

"Then don't have sex. Blow off some steam—dip your toe back into the pool, so to speak. God knows you've pined for your non-boyfriend for long enough."

The final blow hit her square in the chest. She hated how memories of Joss had ruined her for all scening. "I'll miss Tiger's feeding time—"

"The cat is obese. He can survive for an extra couple of hours, if not a few days. I think you should give this one-night stand a shot. As far as safe environments go, the club can't be beat."

Chuckling, Kim placed her hands on her hips. "Why are you so gung-ho about my date? Your sex life is even worse than mine." She'd bet good money the nerdy sub was a virgin.

"Hey, I have online sex on a regular basis, with the same Dom, and we've been exclusive for *months*—an eternity in millennial time. It's as healthy as digital relationships get. Besides, Madame Eve has an insane hook-up to commitment conversion rate, or so I've heard. I need you to use her service and report back. It might help me perfect my app's algorithm."

"So you're sacrificing me on the altar of your coding glory?"

"Pretty much." Moni batted her long, sooty lashes. "Remember all those times you had me swing by your place to feed your damn kitty? I'm cashing the favors in."

To be fair, the woman had begged for pet-sitting opportunities and was responsible for Tiger's excessive toy collection. "I don't think—"

"White Rabbit chewy candy. Half a pound.

Brought from Chinatown to you at the beginning of your shift tomorrow. All you have to do is show up for this date, stay for at least five minutes, and give me the deets."

Kim's molars clicked together. As far as bribes went, her favorite dessert happened to be a potent brand of catnip.

Chapter Three

Kim squinted as she shuffled through the elevator doors. The subterranean level housing the interrogation room had adopted a catacomb-like appearance for the week, with faux stone façades covering the hallway walls and grayish brown carpeting lining the floor. Perhaps to mask the temporary decor's lack of authenticity, the sconces had been dimmed to their lowest setting and covered with black shades.

The perfect lighting for capture games, or a nice long nap.

Given a choice, she'd opt for the latter. Sleep-deprived, she'd struggled to keep her eyes open long before midnight. At 3:00 a.m., her waking fantasy involved a soft mattress, purring cat, and plush comforter. Heck, at this stage, a clean floor and rolled-up jacket would more than do. Yawning, she trudged to the section's check-in station. If everything proceeded according to plan, she might set a record for shortest blind date.

Upon discerning the hostess' features, her mood tanked. Of course, the pesky control-freak wouldn't leave their fact-finding mission up to chance. "Moni, why the heck are you wearing a dungeon monitor uniform?"

Though clad in a white button down, red vest, crimson armband, and black pants, the woman's curves and diminutive height guaranteed her status as the least intimidating DM in Carnivore Club history. Kim had shouldered the title for about two weeks, until she'd face-planted a six-foot-something troublemaker in the middle of a bar full of exhibitionists. In fights, well-timed maneuvers and speed trumped brute strength, assuming the willingness to do real damage.

For this reason, she'd followed up the takedown with a hard stomp on the balls, eliminating the threat until hotel security arrived. The decision had cemented her reputation as a staff member with whom one should not fuck.

One person must have missed the memo. "I traded shifts with Billy." Moni's crocodile smile bared two rows of gleaming white teeth. "Good thing, too. You're in blatant violation of the dress code. You can't initiate a scene in uniform. It's against the rules."

"Which is why I ditched the branded accessories." Kim gestured at her arm and torso. "On the topic of rules, your traipsing around in that vest is worse. You're a bartender. If a situation got sticky, what are you going to do, make everyone a drink?"

"Not a bad idea. Besides"—the temporary DM patted her enviably lush butt—"a crap load of cardio-kickboxing classes went into this booty. My high kick is a thing to behold."

When Kim scowled, the geek hastily added, "Geez,

tone down the cranks, would ya? I convinced the real monitor to leave for fifteen minutes—enough time for me to enforce basic club etiquette. You're a sub. Cleavage is required. Chop, chop."

"For the love of— Fine." Too sleepy to argue, Kim tugged at the top buttons of her uniform. She didn't have much in the way of breasts, and her sports bra reduced cleavage to a mere technicality. "Happy?"

Tapping a laminated black card on her palm, the self-appointed enforcer clucked. "You're cheating, but let's move on. It says here submissives may cover no more than forty percent of their bodies while on this floor. You're hovering at around seventy. Pull out your shirttails and tie them under those tata-tamers. By the way, who invented that bra? Sadists?"

"Could be." Having devoted a significant portion of her workouts to abdominal exercises, baring her midriff didn't strike Kim as a huge deal. When her friend's eyes widened at the sight of her four pack, she patted her tummy. "I have non-existent boobs and buns. It gives me fewer body parts to focus on."

"Since my ass inflates if I even smell chocolate, you get no sympathy. Speaking of butts, I'm afraid those pants must go. The shoes, too. With chases going on, we're enforcing a barefoot policy. Best to keep the floors as clean as possible. Lots of members get their faces smushed on this carpet. Even with steam-cleaning between rounds, footwear is a no-no."

"There's a reason I don't like coming this far below ground." With a shudder, she yanked off her boots. "Some of the role-play veers into creepy territory."

"Liar. You completed a profile on my app, remember? I know all your kinks. Capture games are one of your faves, though you've never tried one out.

Tonight's as good a time as any."

"I thought user data was private," she sputtered.

"Not in the beta testing phase. Didn't you read the fine print? Hey, don't look at me like that. I'm the last person who'd judge." With a cluck, Moni retrieved the boots. "Bedroom tastes are just that—*tastes*. My favorite ice-cream flavor doesn't say anything about my psyche. Neither does my limit list. On an unrelated note, take off your pants."

"I'm not meeting my date in underwear." Kim huffed. "The bottoms stay."

Like a magician, her friend whipped out a pleated skirt from behind the check-in station. "Good thing I'd planned around your prudishness. Get with the times, lady. Tis the age of 'Free the Nipple' campaigns, and you live in Vegas."

"Says the girl whose wardrobe consists of oversized T-shirts and baggy jeans." After losing a brief staring contest, Kim wiggled out of her trousers. "You're such a hypocrite."

"Hey, I'd bring on the sexy if I could. But I'm a female with coding skills. Most of my work-friends are man-children who never get laid. If they catch even a whiff of hotness, I lose all respect." Flashing a wide grin, the woman lifted her palm for a high-five. "Did we ace the slutty cosplayer look, or what? You even have braids."

Kim tugged the skirt another quarter inch down her hips. The hem barely grazed the back of her thighs. Overdue for an afternoon at the Laundromat, she'd been forced to wear pink lacy panties. "Braid— singular." She'd coiled the thick rope of hair around her head to keep it out of the way. "And no, I'm not switching to pigtails. One more attempt at a vicarious sex life from you, and I'm heading home. You'd better double the candy bribe, by the way. I've gone above and beyond the call of duty to investigate your competition."

"Mercenary, aren't you?" With an exaggerated bow, Moni ushered her in. "I always pay my debts, and any candy I snag from you doesn't count toward my calorie limit. I'll even swing by to feed your cat after I leave. Run along. And knock your mystery Dom dead."

Navigating the meandering hallway on autopilot, Kim pondered a literal interpretation of her friend's advice. If she started the meeting with a strong right hook, she'd be home free in five seconds flat.

The idea began to lose its appeal as the charged atmosphere colored her awareness. Though the low lighting left most of the area obscured, evidence of illicit games bombarded her—pounding footsteps, high-pitched cries, thumps as falling bodies vibrated the floor.

Her breaths turned shallow. The service couldn't have picked a setting more in sync with her peculiar tastes. The fabricated sense of danger sped up her pulse. Adrenaline pushed back tiredness. She couldn't ignore the excited screams, shadowed struggles, and the scent of sex and sweat. Her ears pricked at the rhythmic smack of flesh against flesh, the muffled moans of gagged subs, the loud cracks as crops met skin. Harsh pants, metallic clinks, and hisses of airborne leather added percussion to the erotic symphony.

Despite her recent brush with danger, she still fantasized about being chased, caught, and dominated. Each night, she dreamt of the same man pinning her to the ground, stared into his merciless green eyes as he pried her legs apart and forced his way inside her.

Her fingertips tingled by the time she reached the interrogation room. Sucking air into her lungs, she flattened her palms on the entryway. Regaining equilibrium through the slight chill, she focused on spacing out her breaths. Her nipples might have tightened to painful peaks, moisture might coat her palms, but she had no doubt she'd spend the night alone.

The Dom she wanted to play with resided on the opposite end of the continent. Even if he were right in front of her, she wouldn't—couldn't—allow their lives to tangle again.

Squaring her shoulders, she turned the knob and pushed the heavy slab. The ground dropped out from under her the moment she spotted her date's familiar reflection in the two-way mirror.

Joss's mouth curved, the smile grooving his stubbled jaw. White cuffs peeked out from the ends of his gray jacket sleeves. Silvery links glinted under the white, fluorescent light. With his pale hair tied in a queue at his nape and his collar open, he embodied a modern-day Viking.

"I come in peace." He lifted his wrists, which were handcuffed together and chained to a metal ring on the floor. Full of mischief, his jade eyes sparkled. Her reaction to his playful salutation brought an unwelcome realization. Time hadn't muted the bond between them, their sizzling chemistry all the more potent because of the months spent apart.

The sight of him shattered her defenses. Trouble in an expensive suit, he'd worn the same wicked expression when they'd met. It was her first day working as a hostess at a BDSM club in Boston. They'd chatted, he'd swung by her station a few times, and, after her shift, he'd materialized with a piping-hot pumpkin spice latte in hand.

Even then, she'd suspected him to be more than he seemed—a ruthless man wearing the mask of a dilettante. She should have walked away, should have trusted her instincts and steered clear of someone so far out of her league. While claiming to be a corporate errand boy, he'd drawn attention wherever they'd gone, his charisma as palpable as the crisp scent of his expensive cologne.

But the heartbreaking loneliness she'd sensed had stretched their walk into a stroll along the Charles, a harmless coffee into hours of conversation and laughter. Despite her misgivings, they'd become friends. That step, she'd never regret.

"What are you doing here?" The impulse to throw her arms around his broad shoulders an obsession, she rooted her heels to the floor. All dreams must end. Hers did months ago.

Why, then, did it feel as if a new one was about to begin?

Her date pulled a rolled up piece of paper from his breast pocket. "What I do best—negotiating. You see, I have a hostage. Your cat has been relocated to my suite. Unless we come to terms, I'm shipping him back to Boston."

Sucker-punched by his threat, she stomped to his side. Protective rage scattered dark splotches across her vision. "You *kidnapped* my cat?"

"The legalities are debatable." He smoothed out the giant, glossy printout, time-stamped for less than half an hour ago. It showed Tiger on a humongous bed, surrounded by silky throw pillows. A plate of what looked like smoked salmon had captured the little traitor's complete attention. "You see, he's yours, and you're mine, making me his owner by extension. I'm taking care of what belongs to me. Besides, he's enjoying himself."

The heavy door swung shut behind her. The unexpected claim, one blurted out with the casualness of a discussion about weather, robbed her of words. Though they'd burned up the sheets together countless times, they'd both taken great care to keep things light. "But.... Since when...?"

"Since always."

The man must have suffered some sort of brain injury in the past ten months. She shook her head, half certain she'd conked out during the walk here and was dreaming the entire meeting. "Even back then, we were *friends with benefits*."

"I never confirmed anything of the sort. I can't help it if you keep jumping to idiotic conclusions."

The man could be such a lawyer. Despite the warmth spreading inside her chest, she crossed her arms. "Commitment has to go both ways. I never agreed to belong to you."

"I beg to differ. Remember what you said that time in my car?"

At the reminder, her cheeks flamed. After getting into a huge fight on their drive back from Martha's Vineyard, he'd parked in a secluded lot and put the SUV's seatbelt to creative use. After forcing several orgasms on her, he'd dragged her outside to fuck her against the hood.

Angry sex with a cranky Dom had left her sore the

next day. More than once during the rough night, she'd obeyed his order and screamed "I'm yours."

At war with her traitorous body, she focused on the cold tile lining the interrogation room, a stark contrast to the carpet outside. The jacked-up AC had turned the confined space into a refrigerator. Chilled air continued to pour in from the vents above. Nonetheless, her shirt resembled a straightjacket, her scant clothing enveloping her in stifling heat.

His gaze drifted to her chest. With her boobs strapped down, there wasn't much to see. Nonetheless, he licked his lips. "Your memory's in working order, at least. Why don't you get rid of your top? You'll end up naked sooner or later."

Firming her mouth into a line, she circled to the other side of the stainless steel table. Without something physical separating them, she might lose her mind completely and kiss him. "Don't talk to me like that. We're not in a scene."

"Aren't we?" His piercing gaze bored into hers, the unblinking scrutiny sending a shiver down her spine. She shuffled back until her heel met the wall. Goose bumps pricked her exposed nape. She'd forgotten how the laid-back playboy could slip into Dominant mode from one blink to the next.

Shaking off the urge to give him what they both wanted, she rested the back of her head against the mirror. "No, we're not. And Hell will freeze before I let you take Tiger."

"How about this?" Rolling it back up, he tapped the stiff photo paper against his palm. "I'll give him back, but I get to visit whenever I want. We can arrange sleepovers."

Fighting flashbacks of waking up in his strong

arms, she marched forward, reached across the table, and yanked the blackmail tool out of his hand. "Is everything a game to you?"

"No. I only play with people I care about." In a lightning-fast move, he captured her wrist. "It's nice touching you again."

Comfort from the skin-on-skin contact spun her head. Until he'd caught her, they'd been on even ground. The warmth seeping from his palm put her at a distinct disadvantage.

She'd wanted him then. She wanted him now. *Damn it.*

Bending at the waist to further her reach, she smacked the side of his head with the photo. "The feeling's not mutual. Let me go."

"Liar." He tightened his grip. "Kiss me already. You know you want to."

"In your dreams."

"It's a recurring one." When he glanced over her shoulder, her throat dried up. How had he tricked her into bending above the table, with her butt sticking out and a two-way mirror behind her?

"Stop staring at my panties," she rasped. "Is there anyone on the other side?" Exhibitionists often used the interrogation room for public display. At the press of a button, the glass could clear to reveal an audience. She knew from firsthand experience he enjoyed both watching and being watched.

A typical man, his gaze reverted to her boobs. "What do you think?"

Her heart thudded. "Joss, don't—"

"Why not?" He kissed the heel of her hand, his tongue circling the pulse point on her wrist. When he pressed his teeth into her and sucked, she fought back a moan.

"You're wet," he murmured.

With a squeak, she clamped her thighs together.

At his chuckle, she groaned. Damn the man and his bluffs. Her reaction alone confirmed his observation as truth.

A jarring snick shattered her spiral of embarrassment. In a flash, cold metal replaced his fingers. When she glanced up, his hands were free, and he'd snapped the other end of the handcuffs to a bondage loop welded to the corner of the table.

Furious at herself for letting this happen, she aimed her makeshift weapon at his face. He caught the blow long before impact, using his superior strength to force her arm down. Pulling a matching pair of cuffs from his back pocket, he shackled her wrist to the opposite corner before prying the photo from her hand.

He'd played her. Every move, from the moment she'd stepped through the door, had been one long distraction.

"You're off your game." He tapped her chin with the makeshift baton. "Didn't think I'd get the jump on you this fast."

The restraints forced her prone against the cold metal, the table's width allowing next to no bend in her arms. Spine arched and butt up, she was flashing the mirror and whoever watched on the other side.

The realization should have triggered embarrassment. Instead, it aroused. *Shit*. After ten months of sexual frustration, her body refused to cooperate with her brain.

The edge of the baton shifted to her cheek. "You've lost weight. When was the last time you slept?"

"Bite me."

"Oh, I will. I'd planned on talking through our issues *before* tying you up. But you made reversing the order too tempting." Gripping the back of her shirt collar, he jerked her an inch off the table, stretching her arms until the restraints dug into skin. "The last time we played with cuffs, I used leather and fur. Tonight, I won't go so easy. You haven't been taking care of yourself. I'll have to punish you."

Liquid fire dampened her panties. He liked it rough. He liked this game. So did she.

"Go to hell."

"But I've just escaped. Since we've dispensed with the bondage, you choose. Sex first, or talk first?"

She ground her molars together hard enough her jaw hurt. "We have nothing to talk about."

"Sex it is. Might as well take the edge off." He slid his hand to her nape, the contact both a comfort and threat. With his thumb at her jugular, he could render her unconscious with little effort. "What's the club's safe word?"

Biting her lower lip, she fought a wave of mortification. Of course, he wouldn't allow her the pretense. They were scening. They'd started the moment she'd stepped through the door of her own free will.

And she didn't want to stop. Not yet. "Red."

"Unoriginal, but it'll do." Folding at the waist, he caught her lower lip between his teeth. The kiss was gentle, teasing, a stark contrast to the solid manacles holding her prisoner. The cuffs lacked the customary lining for BDSM play. Any struggle would break skin, leaving her no choice but to hold still.

His grip on her the only other point of contact, he

slid his tongue along the seam of her mouth. He coaxed, rather than pushed, tempting her with pleasure until she let him in. Refusing to allow him control of the kiss, she pushed back, sucking and nipping until the slow, steady caresses escalated to a sensual duel.

A loud crack—the cursed photo hitting the floor. Less than a second later, his other hand burned her cheek. Her head imprisoned, she couldn't move as his teeth scraped her raw, the devouring kiss establishing beyond question who held the reins.

Sweat coated her limbs as he mastered her with the confidence of an experienced Dom. One by one, he plucked off the pins holding her hair in place. With the room dead quiet, the metal bobs clicked as they hit the tile. He unraveled her braid, spreading the slippery tresses over her shoulders and back.

Breaking the kiss, he clutched a handful, tugging hard enough tears fogged her eyes. At the sharp sting, what little remained of her resistance splintered.

Surrender edged out thought. Later, they'd talk. Later, she'd worry about her next move. After close to a year apart, they deserved to steal a moment of pure pleasure.

"Good girl." He tightened his grip, his approval distracting from the pain. He fed her his thumb, and she watched his fly tent as she sucked and licked. Whenever she paused to draw in a breath, he yanked her head back, punishing her for stalling without permission.

Their breaths quickened to pants. Despite the freezing table and nippy air, an electric storm burned her from within, her hunger for his touch a torture beyond measure. When he finally let her go, she was gulping for air. By the time her lungs settled, he'd padded around her and flipped up her skirt.

She whimpered, all too aware of the view she presented. He'd never given her a straight answer about an audience.

"Remember how I punished you for lying to me?"

Past and present merged. The last time he'd positioned her this way, he'd driven her to orgasm in a lounge full of people. "Omission isn't a lie." If she'd told him about her complete lack of experience, he'd never have scened with her in public. She'd wanted her first time to be memorable.

"That's what I keep telling you." He yanked down her panties, leaving them circling her ankles as he stepped closer. Shoving his hand between her shaking legs, he growled, "You kept shaving. Good. Everyone is about to see what a hard spanking does to you."

Horrified and aroused, she gritted her teeth as he swatted her, over and over until she quivered from the delicious throb. All the while, his fingers rested on her unprotected flesh, unmoving even as slickness betrayed her increasing need.

"I hate you." She squirmed against his hand, desperate for more contact, more pressure, more everything.

"We need to work on your honesty." He hit her harder, and his fingers refused to move. "Tell me the truth. I'll let you come."

She squeezed her eyes shut. "Kiss my ass."

"Well, since you asked nice." He stopped so abruptly the shock sent her sagging against the restraints. The cuffs' bite forced her shoulders up as his hot breath spread pleasure throughout her abused bottom. Then he bit her, hard enough she jumped in place.

She growled at his laugh, fought a moan as his teeth unclamped. He sucked her burning flesh, his circling tongue tormenting her with ripples of need. He lingered long enough to mark her skin, to leave behind the kind of brand that would haunt her for days.

"Joss...." She gasped. "Stop playing."

He released her after one last, playful nip. His hand between her shoulder blades, he shoved her down. "All this lip from such a tiny sub. I guess I should remind you who's in charge."

Cold leather and rounded metal brushed her flaming butt. Rustles and clinks heralded a zipper's whirr. The faint scent of citrus followed the crackle of a packet tearing.

She shifted her hips in a bid to escape. He planned to take her like this, with little more than a kiss as foreplay. After all this time, it would hurt—each penetration equal parts punishment and pleasure.

And she'd die if he stopped.

He insinuated his hand between her legs. Parting her labia with his middle finger, he rubbed until more moisture betrayed her eagerness, all the while avoiding her clit. Refusing to give him the satisfaction, she clamped her mouth shut as he pushed inside. The friction spread fire across every inch of her skin.

"God, I'd forgotten how tight you are." When he added a finger and pushed deeper, her inner muscles contracted in an instinctive attempt to slow his invasion. Choking on a cry, she blinked away tears of frustration as he pumped his fingers in and out. He kept his strokes slow, languorous, and maddening, the painful impalement coiling fear and anticipation into a rope of desire.

She wanted more. She wanted *him*. But he was bigger—so much bigger than this.

"You'll take me. You'll take all of me." His knuckles scraped her as he pulled out, the abrasion turning her legs to jelly. "And you'll fucking like it."

His withdrawal left her drowning in need. An eternity passed in the second before his erection warmed her inner thighs. He grabbed her hips, lifting her until her toes hovered above the tile.

His hard thrust robbed her lungs of air. He held her captive, angling her to accept an even deeper penetration. Twisting her wrist, she gripped the handcuffs' chains. She clung to the metal restraints, needing an anchor as he quickened his rhythm. Each entry was a mark of possession, a lance of pain and pleasure she had no choice but to endure.

With a muttered curse, he shifted his hold, looping one arm around her waist to hold her in place. His other hand drifted to her belly, reaching lower until it reached the point where their bodies met. He circled her clit, the contact sending an electric jolt through her core. Her muscles spasmed, her toes curling as the dual strokes propelled her toward a blazing euphoria.

Utter powerlessness. The heady rush of submission made each impalement easier than the one before. She bit her lip hard enough to taste blood, held back a scream for as long as she could. Then awareness shattered, splintering her world into shards of silver.

Chapter Four

K im woke in a cocoon of hard muscle and minty cologne. Joss's thighs warmed her sore butt. His arms caged her shoulders. Squeezing her eyes shut, she snuggled closer, refusing to wake from the best dream in recent memory.

"Cute as this is, I'm bored. You're awake. Entertain me." Warm fingers patted her cheek. She grunted. Leave it to her subconscious to incorporate her cat's wake-up routine into the dream.

A pair of knuckles squeezed her nose. With a gasp, she forced her lids to unstick. Tiger must be sitting on her face again.

Reality and fantasy realigned as she blinked away the cobwebs. Full consciousness accompanied an unsettling discovery. "Where the hell are my panties?"

"In a safe place." Grabbing her shoulders, the man-sized feline forced her into a seated position. When her lids drooped, he shook her hard enough to rattle her teeth. "I should have guessed you'd conk out. Sex always makes you sleepy. But this time, you

46

dozed longer than usual. My pecs started to fall asleep. I didn't know they could."

They sprawled in one corner of the interrogation room. Fluorescent light blazed from above, illuminating the handcuffs fastened to the table. She could see through the giant two-way mirror on the far wall. Spotting the empty rows of chairs on the other side, she hid her face in the crook of his arm. "Oh God. That didn't just happen."

"You've slept for"—he checked his wristwatch—"two hours or so. As I said, numb chest. Worth it though. You're a lot prettier without dark circles under your eyes."

The soreness between her legs an uncomfortable reminder of her recent lapse in judgment, she swallowed to soothe her parched throat. Not ready to discuss what they'd done or face the ramifications, she focused her attention on his jacket. "How can you wear a wool suit in Las Vegas?"

"I plan my day around air-conditioning. If there's strenuous physical activity on the agenda, I try to make the ambient temperature close to freezing." He pressed something cold and wet against the back of her neck. She turned her head to discover a bottle of Perrier. Someone must have delivered it while she was out.

"Which explains this ice box." Yanking the fizzy water out of his grasp, she guzzled the icy liquid. Unflavored soda had no reason for existing, but thirst overruled her picky taste buds. "So you came knowing I'd let you fuck me." It hurt her pride he'd deemed her a sure thing.

"I *hoped* missing me would throw you off balance." He retrieved the half-empty bottle and placed it to their side. "That and threatening to steal the damn cat. And yes, from the moment we met, getting your panties off was always the simple part. Everything else is a shit ton more complicated."

A way with words, the man had not. Too bad his brand of dominance chimed perfectly with her needs. "Yeah, I'm easy."

"You're the opposite of easy, pet. Taking care of you redefined difficult." A grin creased his cheeks. "But I don't mind. You're worth it."

She heaved a sigh. Staying mad suddenly became impossible.

With great effort, she rekindled her anger. "You lied to me. I'm not okay with it, although I should have guessed you weren't some lackey." In the posh surroundings of Boston's underground BDSM club, Joss had commanded obedience with too much confidence, shirked the trappings of privilege with the callousness of a man who'd wanted for nothing. But she'd seen what she'd wanted to see, blinding herself to a truth so obvious the charade seemed laughable. "Personal assistant my ass."

"As I said, you jump to the weirdest conclusions." Lacing his fingers through her hair, he combed the tangled strands apart. "To be fair, my brother did consider me his personal assistant. He just never paid me. Come to think of it, the cash always flowed the other way round. By the time you'd caught on, you liked instant messaging me between classes too much to ask questions."

"Fine. I don't make friends easily, and I didn't want to lose you." She respected herself enough to admit it out loud. "But why pretend to be someone else?" Obscene wealth was an asset, not a handicap.

His icy mask cracked. "I got addicted to the way you look at me."

She frowned. "What way?"

"As if I'm a person, not a name. Before telling you the truth, I wanted to become someone you could like."

Traces of past pain furrowed his forehead. With trembling fingers, she smoothed out the grooves. "You're already someone I like." Someone she more than liked. "No matter what happens, you need to know that."

He caught her hand and brought it to his lips. "Still think you can run from this, do you?"

She had to. "When I do, I need you to remember it's because of *me*."

"God damn. I'm getting the 'it's not you it's me' speech." He drew air quotes with his fingers. "It must be karma. Nice try, but there is a logical flaw to your breakup routine. You see, *I* decide how I feel about you. *You* decide how you feel about me. How one feels about oneself at no point factors into the equation."

His argument made her dizzy. "Were you on the debate team or something?"

"Parliamentary and forensic. Trust me, you can't win." Behind his smug smile, she glimpsed something more—obstinate determination and absolute certainty.

Thrilled and terrified, she swallowed the lump in her throat. "We could get over each other if we tried."

Imprisoning her with his arms, he trailed his nose down the line of her neck. "How's that working out for you? On my end, every hot chick I see has your face. One look at your reflection, and bam—instant hard on. Our breather flopped." He dipped his head lower, scattering kisses along her collarbones. "I'm glad it's done."

"No." Her vision misted with pulses of crimson. She tried to summon an iota of reluctance. Her libido refused to play ball. "We're not doing this again."

He bit the sensitive spot between her shoulder and neck. "You don't have a choice. I'm calling the shots."

His confidence curled her toes. "What we had was less than a fling." She poured what little willpower she had into the false words.

He squeezed her breast, the proprietary caress arching her back. "You're going to pay for that lie with a lot more than a hard spanking."

Arousal flared, potent and irresistible. "You have no right. I'm not your sub." When he pinched her nipples, flashes of heat threatened to melt away thought. "But there's a whole club full of women willing to play your games."

"I've already chosen mine." She writhed when his grip tightened. In her moment of distraction, he slid his hand under her skirt. With her underwear gone, he could shove his fingers inside her without preamble.

"Joss...." It hurt. In the best way.

He looped his other arm around her. Caught in a vise, she had little recourse beyond a whimpered protest. "I don't want this." But she did. Enough to erase the safe word from her vocabulary.

"Dishonesty seems to be a chronic problem." He pressed down on her clit with his thumb and screwed his digits deeper into her. Her clenching inner muscles supported his observation. So did her uncontrollable spasms as his unyielding penetration vaulted her toward a crest.

She dug her nails into his forearms, a useless defense that only reinforced her helplessness. "Stop it."

He ignored her resistance, playing her like an instrument until sweat once more coated her skin. "Why? You're more honest right after you come."

He added a third finger, and the painful stretching proved too much. She firmed her lips, unwilling to give him the satisfaction of her cries. With her body imprisoned, his ruthless mastery fulfilled one of her darkest fantasies. He forced the orgasm on her, and she wanted it too badly to end their game.

Slumping against his chest, she watched him lick his fingers. God, she'd been easy. Twice in less than three hours.

"It would be my pleasure to keep this up until you tell me what the hell is going on. The truth, or I'll drag you outside and show everyone how wet you are."

Her head spinning from the aftermath of guilty ecstasy, she failed to stop the words from slipping out. "Damn it, Joss. Leave me alone. Go find someone who deserves you. I'm not worth your time"

"What?" The fact that he loosened his arms and allowed her to wiggle free was a testament to his shock. "*Seriously*?"

"It's true." Burning streaks leaked from the corners of her eyes. She had to push him away—for his own good. Scrambling to her feet, she raced to the door. The world spun. She'd gotten up too quickly.

Gripping the handle, she forced herself to remain upright. When she pulled, it refused to budge. "Let me the hell out."

Stunned by Kim's revelation, Joss followed her. He made a living off reading people. The skill worked best face-to-face, or he would have saved himself a trip to this hellhole of heat and never-ending crowds.

On the phone, she'd halfway convinced him she hated his guts. But this wasn't about what he'd done or the hell his family had rained down on her. He had no clue what her problem was, but it had nothing to do with him.

An oppressive weight lifted off his shoulders. Stepping back to give her space, he lifted his hands in a gesture of surrender and took stock of his advantages. He just dragged her through a physical and emotional whirlwind. Despite the nap, she was tired and sleep-deprived.

She couldn't be thinking straight. He would bet his life on it.

If he wanted to ferret out the truth, the moment couldn't be more perfect. "Take a breath. I'm nowhere near you."

She pounded her palms on the door. "Let. Me. Out."

"No. We need to talk. For real, this time." Since she had yet to use the safe word, some part of her must agree.

Straightening her shoulders, she smoothed her skirt and whirled to face him. A pity. He rather enjoyed watching her butt cheeks as she vibrated with frustration.

"Fine. For real—we're done. I can't get over the past. It's time we go our separate ways."

With great difficulty, he forced his gaze away from

the slight sheen between her thighs. Minutes before, her pussy had been milking his fingers, her lithe body writhing on his lap. Chest heaving and cheeks pink, his confused little sub embodied temptation. His dick insisted he shove her against the damn door and fuck her hard. After enough orgasms, she'd come around. She always did.

His brain advised an alternative approach. Whatever her issue was, sex hadn't solved it. Time to switch tactics.

"Bullshit." He crossed his arms. "You've forgiven me. You're not even angry."

"I'm plenty mad, you overconfident asshat."

Clarity smacked him in the face. This wasn't her pissed off face. It was her insecure face.

When he stepped forward, she scuttled back, her tiny feet shifting to a fighting stance. His boner reared painfully against his zipper. Few things turned him on as much as her scratching and biting. The games they played would make her hot and slick. But no matter how horny he got her, their size difference meant fucking could never be easy.

He'd never liked easy.

"You said I deserve someone better. Care to clarify?"

"No." Her voice trembled. "Drop it."

Something had happened the night she ran, something that spooked her so much she refused to stop. He wasn't sure if even *she* knew the reasons behind her actions, but he planned on figuring them out ASAP. Especially if it meant tying her up and interrogating her for hours.

At the thought, more blood pooled to his groin. Zipping up had been a horrible decision.

Her gaze dropped to his crotch. "Don't even think about it." She pointed at the table. "*That* was the absolute last time we will have sex."

"Then why do you keep glancing at the cuffs like you want an encore?" At the reminder of how red her ass had turned, of her delicious moans as he'd hammered into her, his boner grew to the point of extreme discomfort. One scene a night had never been enough. After months of abstinence, he could keep her under him all weekend and want more.

Reaching her side in a single lunge, he caught her chin and tipped her head back. "Can we skip to the part where you tell me what's cooking in your oversized brain? My dick is about to explode."

"Words to melt any girl's panties," she snapped. "Stop telling me what to do."

He dropped a kiss on her stubborn nose. "But it turns you on. Instantly. As for the panties, the task's already done." He'd kept the scraps of pink lace as a souvenir, tucked inside his breast pocket. "The bra is a work in progress."

"Why won't you *listen*?" She stomped her foot. "You wasted a trip. You don't want someone like me. You're hot. You're rich. And, very very *very* deep down, you're a nice person. I'm none of those things. You can do better, and it's only a matter of time before you realize it."

Another slip. Good. For some reason, him crowding her threw her off balance. Beneath her bravado, he sensed fear. The real kind. "Careful sweetheart, you might destroy my courtroom cred. People say I'm a shark, and I like it that way. And you're wrong on two out of three. You're hot and nice—"

"No, I'm not nice. Why does everyone keep saying I'm fucking nice?"

He'd hit a nerve. At her death glare, he dropped the lighthearted pretense. "You're ashamed."

Judging from her gaping mouth, he'd hit the nail on the head. "All this time, you've been protecting me from yourself." The idea refused to sink in. He was the one who'd screwed up. He was the one with enough baggage to sink a ship.

"What if I am?"

He gritted his teeth. His little darling was about to learn the repercussions of taking important decisions into her own misguided hands. Of all the people in this world, she had *nothing* to be ashamed about.

"You let me believe you hated my guts." Try as he might, he couldn't stop his voice from rising several decibels. "You told me to take a hike. All this, because you think *you* aren't good enough for *me?*"

When he grabbed her shoulders, her expression went blank. Pivoting on one foot, she sliced her arm in the air and detached his grip. Sliding her palm along his forearm, she caught his wrist and twisted his hand in, while bending her knees to force him into a lock.

Good thing they'd taken the same martial arts classes. Anticipating her move, he broke free with a hard yank. Taking advantage of his longer legs, he circled her. When she spun, he caught her punch, intercepted her knee, before imprisoning her ankle and launching her back. She turned in time to hit the floor on her hands.

In the split second he hesitated, she kicked his legs out from under him. By the time his ass hit the floor, she'd straddled his waist, her arm bent and ready to strike. A blow to the neck or face would knock him out cold.

Her fist failed to land. Breaths coming in violent gasps, she stalled, and he watched mindless terror leak from her face. As he stared into her haunted eyes, he relived the night he'd raced to save her, only to find her on top of a disarmed assailant, the man's oversized pistol in her tiny hands.

Panic had a death grip on his heart as he'd spotted the two bastards looming behind her, their weapons hovering in the freezing air, inches from her head.

"I would have pulled the trigger." Her whispered confession hurled him to the present, and the horror he glimpsed helped gather the final pieces of the puzzle together. "If you hadn't showed up, I would have murdered a man."

Though most likely the worst move, he dropped his head back. His shoulders shook. His diaphragm inflated enough to bounce her up and down.

"Are you *laughing* at me?"

With a fist hovering above his nose, testing her restraint might not be the wisest move. He caught her waist and reversed their positions, ignoring her high-pitched yelp as he pinned her wrists to either side of her head.

He tried to kiss her, but snapping teeth forced him to abort. "Yep. You're such a goody-two-shoes, it's ridiculous."

She tried to free her arms, but she'd lost her chance to best him when she'd failed to land the final blow. Though quicker, faster, and better trained, she couldn't win a pure match of strength. "I work at a BDSM club." She wrinkled her nose. "I let you fuck me in front of an audience."

"Which proves you're a good girl with kinky tastes." He rolled his eyes. "You've been beating yourself up because you could have killed the man hired to murder you. I wouldn't be surprised if you help little old ladies cross the street."

Her teeth clicked. Note to self—never vacation in retirement hotspots.

The woman needed a devil on her shoulder. Good thing he'd permanently carved room in his schedule to corrupt her. "So, you don't think we should hang out anymore because you're a *horrible* human being who would have shot someone in self-defense but stopped in the nick of time." He tightened his grip. "Thanks for the sentiment, but perhaps you can let me handle the decision-making in this relationship going forward."

"We're not in a relationship." When losing an argument, she always opted for redirection. Three, two, o— "And it's not the *only* reason. There are tons of reasons. If you haven't noticed, I can't afford to shop at Neiman Marcus. I didn't go to some fancy Ivy League school. In this economy, my job prospects aren't rosy. On top of it all, I'm one step up from being a murderer. Trust me, you and I—it won't work."

"What makes you think I care about any of those things?" He could talk her down from the other issues later, but her guilt was unacceptable. "And you're light years away from being a murderer. If I could have gotten away with it, I would have killed all three of those bastards for what they tried to pull. Does that mean I'm a bad person?"

"Of course not. I—"

"I make you happy. You deserve to be happy.

Anyone who says otherwise should be spanked, yourself included. It's obvious the trauma warped your brain. Not too much, but enough to be annoying. We need to fix it, stat."

Her cheeks puffed out. "You're not a psychiatrist."

He tapped her temple. "As I said, this is only a slightly messed up noggin. I know you better than most people. I was also there that night. It was self-defense. You were alone, facing three armed men. Even if you pulled the trigger, you would be in the clear—legally and morally. There, are you cured yet?"

"You don't understand." Her voice turned nasally. *Shit. She'd better not start the waterworks.* He could deal with anything but tears. "When he threw me against the wall.... There was this rush—this thrill. My ears roared. By the time I had him on the ground, my hands weren't shaking. I was ready to kill him. I *wanted* to kill him."

"It was the adrenaline. And your memory is faulty. I saw you on top of him. You were frightened out of your mind."

"No, I wasn't. It's the problem." Gulps of air punctuated her words. "I could take them out. I trained to fight those kinds of attacks. I had no reason to be scared."

Noticing her reddening nose, he groaned. "It's hindsight. Your rational self is looking back in time and inaccurately interpreting the facts." It happened to witnesses all the time, which is why he avoided them in most cases. "Trust me, you were spooked. You had to be. If you want, I'll prove it."

When she blinked, moisture clumped her long lashes into spikes. But no tears leaked out. *Thank God.* "How could you possibly prove something like that?"

After forcing his brain to cycle through the options, he settled on a somewhat unorthodox idea. "If I do, will you let me spend the weekend at your place?"

"I don't think you'd survive." She wrinkled her nose. "You pack your own sheets for overnight stays."

Most people underestimated the value of high thread count Egyptian cotton. "I'll be fine." As long as he stopped at his hotel to grab linens, towels, and toiletries.

"Um...."

"Are you too chicken to accept the bet?"

"Of course not." Her eyes narrowed. "But what do I get if you fail?"

Shit. He'd pulled off too many one-sided deals to sneak another. "I'll give you your cat back." He dangled his ace in the hole. "It's one less thing I can use against you."

Chapter Five

"**A**re you sure you want to do this?"

With a grunt, Joss pulled on the black ski mask a member of the staff had provided. "Of course I am. Why?" The idea of having other men put their hands on Kim made the vein on his forehead tick. But her punishing herself for no reason knotted his gut.

He'd pick angry over nauseous any day of the week.

An identical prop covering his face, Nate crossed his arms. The man wore a dress-shirt the same shade as his blue eyes. Rolled up sleeves revealed tanned arms decorated with tattoos. The pair of snarling dragons had scales mimicking patterns on a microchip. "You're possessive as all hell."

"I can keep a lid on it. If you're worried about your virtual girlfriend getting jealous, you're assisting, not joining the scene." The nerd's only long-term relationship was of the online variety. "If you so much as look at Kim the wrong way, I'll knock out your teeth."

The tech tycoon snorted. "You could *try*. I'm

guessing all your talk about banging a different chick each night was complete bullshit."

"I might have exaggerated a tad." With a sociopathic and unpredictable mother, Joss had learned to embrace habitual misdirection.

"If you're not planning a ménage"—Luka chimed in—"why did you drag our asses here at close to sunrise?"

"I trust you, and you're in town. Besides, you get a kick out of putting poor, defenseless subs on display."

"I watched your *poor, defenseless sub* put my ex's hired muscle in a headlock. Afterwards, she crushed his balls. Now you're asking me to chase her down in a capture game? What if she throat-punches me?" To Joss's disgust, the six-foot-something Dom fidgeted with his collar before shuddering.

"Oh, man up. She's five feet tall and half your weight."

"Luke has a point." Nate cradled his own chin. "And chances are you'll punch us yourself."

Joss tilted his head toward the prep area where Kim stood, her arms extended so a DM could paint fluorescent cuffs on her wrists. The distinctive color assigned to each sub prevented cases of mistaken identity. "She can win a fight with me. She knows it. I want to prove a point, and I need her scared."

"This takes wingman to a whole new level. When Naomi hears about it, and she will, I'll be sharing the couch with our dog." Luka nonetheless pulled on his mask.

Joss nodded his approval. The man's white button-down resembled his own. In the dark, their similar builds should help throw his stubborn sub off-balance. "I sued your psycho ex into bankruptcy, turned you into a rich man, and hooked you up with your current girlfriend. You owe me doesn't quite cut it."

"Fine. But if she breaks my nose, you're paying for plastic surgery. Let's get this done. They're sounding the horn."

Red lights flashed, cloaking the makeshift catacombs in a sinister glow. Recorded thunder accompanied flashes of white light. Even at this hour, quite a few groups had showed up to role-play. Several dungeon monitors patrolled the pathways, on alert for any hint of the safe word or mismatched markers. He, Nate, and Luka wore fluorescent armbands matching the color painted on Kim's wrists and ankles.

When playing close to the line, reputable clubs operated with an abundance of caution.

The subs raced into the darkness, their progress slowed by meandering paths marked by fake boulders and plastic shrubs. He scanned the area for his prize. Hunting instincts and adrenaline took over, lending the theatrical props surprising authenticity.

Heart pounding, he vaulted after his prey, having glimpsed the florescent sheen of her markings out of the corner of his eye. He'd scoped out the area beforehand, needing any advantage he could get. Turned around by false routes and delayed by manmade obstacles, Kim had no hope of escape.

He envisioned looping his arm around her neck, hauling her against him as she fought to break free. She would put up a fight, forcing him to throw her to the ground. Pinned by his weight, she'd struggle as he tore off her clothes, her silky mane framing her naked body as he pried her legs apart. He'd find her wet, her hips lifting to meet his touch.

He hadn't expected her to lay a trap. As they rounded a corner, the sneaky minx appeared out of nowhere, her arms and legs a blur in the dark. She tripped Luka then launched her entire weight at Nate.

She'd put both his friends on their asses in less than a minute. But trouble came in threes. Joss yanked her off Nate by the scruff of her neck, shoving her toward Luka as the man rose to his haunches. She dropped and rolled before he could lock his arms around her waist. Leaping to her feet, she disappeared around the corner with an exuberant laugh.

A strategic mistake.

Until this moment, his friends had been more spectator than participant, her delicate appearance leashing their predatory instincts. Attacking them turned her into a worthy adversary. She'd amped up the stakes.

They all took off, the fluorescent bands on her skin betraying her location and path. Though fast, her short legs couldn't outpace men twice her size. When she glanced back, he caught a glimmer of the blankness he'd witnessed in the interrogation room— the sudden merging of past and present that turned her sprint choppy and erratic.

Bathed in red light, chased by assailants in ski masks, she'd be hard-pressed to keep memories at bay. She stumbled, almost fell, before righting herself and pulling her shoulders back. Spinning to face them, she lifted her chin and fisted her hands, her expression fierce enough he doubted she recognized this as theater.

Aiming for her shirt collar, he shot out his hand. Blocking his attack, she bent her knees and threw her shoulder at his ribs. He twisted to the side in time to avoid injury. Thrown off balance, he deflected her kick, the momentum landing him on the carpet.

She pounced. Her fist would have dented his face had Nate not looped his arm around her neck. She clawed at his hand as he pulled her back, leaving dark lines where nails met skin. He growled, hauling her off the floor so her kicks met air.

She arced her heel back. It hit Nate's shin hard enough he cursed and threw her to the ground. Having waited for this window, Joss jumped on her the moment she landed.

Straddling her, he dug the heels of his palms into her shoulders as Nate and Luka separated to pin her arms and legs. Ignoring the sheen of sweat coating her face and neck, he grabbed the sides of her shirt.

Buttons popped as he tore the garment. Ignoring her desperate struggles, he unhooked the front clasp of her sports bra. Her breasts sprung free, two pale globes turned pink by the crimson light.

She thrashed, twisting her torso in a bid to escape his rough exploration. He pinched her nipples, raked his fingers over her flesh as his friends held her captive. She couldn't move, imprisoned by three men, all bigger and stronger.

His voice a low growl, he unbuckled his belt. "Are you scared?"

Her whimper tore at him, but he kept going, whipping the leather through the loops fast enough it hissed. Sliding down to sit on her knees, he hiked up her skirt. He saw the whites of her eyes as he shoved his palm between her clammy thighs. "So, are you fine? Is everything under control? Do you still want to fuck?"

He pulled his hand away the moment she hissed, "No. No, I'm not fine, all right? Back the hell off."

Tearing off his ski mask, he heaved a relieved breath. He'd put on a good show, but they'd already gone further than he wanted. Cradling her face, he forced her to make eye contact.

Her lower lip trembled. With her pupils dilated, her irises were pools of black. The knot at the pit of his stomach wound tighter. It had to be done, but he didn't have to like it. "You were afraid. So afraid, the game didn't turn you on."

"I told you to back off," she growled.

"That's not what you need." He kissed her, a slow, tender caress aimed at soothing her nerves. When he pulled back, her heaving breaths slowed to a more steady rhythm. Neck muscles relaxing against his fingers, she shut her eyes.

"Were you this scared when those bastards grabbed you?" He had to confirm.

"Quit talking and kiss me again."

"Stop trying to cheat and answer the question."

"Damn it. Fine. With them, it was much worse. So, yeah. I'm an idiot." From her tone, frustrated anger had replaced fear. "But keep rubbing it in, and I'll smack you."

Both Nate and Luka chuckled. They let her go so Joss could scoop her into his arms. When she snuggled closer, his world righted. Comforting her was its own reward.

"And you're back." He kissed her sweat-dampened hair. "Any chance you'll admit I'm right out loud? I want witnesses."

"Don't make me head-butt you." She pinched his triceps. "Point taken. I'm a little messed up. I'll figure out how to get past it later. Right now, I'm dead tired. Let's go home and sleep."

Savoring the casual invitation, he glanced at Luka. Despite the ski mask, he caught the man's wink. A second later, his friend raced off.

"Sleep is for losers. Sure you're all better?"

Nodding, she pushed at his chest. "Yeah. You can take your paws off me. You smell good, but you're squeezing so tight I'm about to suffocate."

"Is this any way to speak to your Dom?" Nate drawled from behind her. For a man who often demanded high protocol, he likely considered scratch marks on his arms a serious offense. "Your sub needs a lesson in manners."

"Agreed." Joss tightened his hold. "All this kicking and biting deserves punishment."

Kim tensed. They'd scened together too many times for her to miss his intent. "I haven't bitten anyone." Her breathless protest was all the permission he needed.

"But she did kick." Luka's drawl announced his return. "She owes us a show. More than one, to be fair." He dropped Joss's toy bag on the floor with a loud thump. Anticipating this end to the night, they'd stashed it nearby.

"Wait." She squirmed, fear leaching into her voice. "Ménage is a hard limit."

"It won't be a ménage." He ran his palm down her back. "They'll watch. They'll hold you down. But anything sexual only happens with me."

Through his shirt, he felt her nipples tightening to sharp points. Oh yes, the idea made her hot. Though

66

neither of them would ever share, they both enjoyed an audience—in this case, a participating one.

Unlocking his arms, he nodded at Nate and Luka. "Prep her."

With a grunt, Nate caught Kim by the hair and yanked her to her feet. He wound his hand in her tresses as Luka stripped off the remainder of her clothing. His movements brusque and efficient, he kept skin contact to a minimum. *Smart man.*

During the entire ordeal, Kim trained her gaze on Joss. As she lost her undergarments, her lips paled to match the color of her skin.

Marching to face her, he placed his knuckle under her chin. "What is bothering you?"

Seconds passed before she answered. "Too many hands. That night...before I broke free, they had me on the pavement. Later, I had nightmares...."

For months, his sleep had also been tormented by visions of her bloodied and broken. "Let's replace the memory with something better." As her Dom, his duty was to give her what she needed. The capture game served a purpose beyond proving his point. "You have a safe word. You're in complete control. This is for your pleasure, no one else's."

With a shaky laugh, she arched a brow. "I'm pretty sure you're enjoying this."

Nate and Luka dragged her to the floor. Manacling her wrists and ankles with their hands, they extended her arms and legs until they had her spread eagle between them. Bared to the skin, she didn't fight their hold.

Joss grabbed his toy bag before kneeling by her waist. He palmed her breast, his fingers marking her skin as he twisted his hand. "I like having you naked and helpless."

She shivered. "And showing me off."

"That, too." When he pulled out a blindfold, she whipped her head left and right.

"Trust me."

Biting her lower lip, she held still as he wound the black silk over her eyes. Having shrouded her in darkness, he reached into his bag. Opening a bottle, he held it in front of her nose. The minty scent wafted up, reminding him of the first time he'd introduced her to chemical play.

"Remember this?" He'd tested the mixture on her delicate skin before, making sure it had no effect beyond the intended.

Her breath hitching, she gave a jerky nod. With her nipples on the small side, clamps weren't his preferred method for tormenting her breasts. He decorated the tips with the slippery liquid, watched as her dusky areolas darkened and ruched. Using more liberal amounts of the balm, he drew swirls along her cleavage, across her taut abs, and down to her navel. When he blew on the pattern, she whimpered.

The icy-hot sting on his finger gave him a good idea of how the compound must be affecting her. By the time he'd spread the heat to her hips and inner thighs, sweat beaded on her chest and chin. "You're wet, and I haven't even touched you."

She tried to squeeze her legs together, failing when Luka tightened his hold. His voice a whip, Nate united her wrists and then reached down to splay his hand around her neck. "Did your Dom give you permission to move?"

Her lips parted before she clamped her mouth

shut with a loud click. She'd held back the safe word. Joss's tensed muscles unlocked. He'd pushed her to the edge of her hard limit, but she'd surrendered the reins to him.

A darker instinct demanded more. Shoving his hand between her spread legs, he dipped his finger inside her.

Wincing, she squirmed. In response, the other two Doms pressed down, acting as immovable restraints.

"She's wet," Nate observed, his words a taunt. "I could eat her up."

"If she doesn't stop moving, I'll let you."

At his empty threat, she went motionless.

Pulling out, Joss coated two fingers with the balm then eased them back inside her. She was tight and hot. The deeper he shoved, the slicker she became.

"Please, don't." She moaned. "You'll make me come." For whatever reason, she had always been shy about others witnessing her pleasure.

He pinched her nipples, squeezing hard enough she cried out. The compound would have sensitized her skin, making her breasts feel swollen and hot. Despite his previous threat, she twisted her torso in an attempt to thwart his fondling. Her disobedience warranted a proportional response.

When he forced an additional finger inside her, her back arched. He pushed harder, neglecting her clit on purpose. After a brief search, the tip of his middle finger met its mark.

Her hips shot up.

Slow and steady, he fingered her, each penetration far enough to hit her sweet spot. He heightened the stimulation by tormenting her breasts, his hard squeezes forcing muffled cries from her pursed lips.

Within seconds, she shuddered.

She whimpered when he yanked his hand from between her legs mid-orgasm. Nate pulled off her blindfold, and her lids fluttered open in time to catch Joss tasting her off his fingers. When her captors freed her, she remained on the floor, her breaths coming in harsh, shallow pants.

Not giving her time to recover, he tugged open his fly and freed his erection. Then he straddled her, positioning his knees on either side of her head. His hand under her nape, he positioned her mouth. When she didn't respond fast enough, he gripped her jaw, forcing her lips to part. "You know what to do."

At his gruff order, she darted her tongue out to taste the drop of moisture on the tip of his cock. Her lids heavy, she surrounded him in sultry warmth, teased him with the barest hint of teeth. His mood too dark for sensual play, he fed her his length, his fingers clutching her silky hair as he forced her to take him all the way.

He rode her, maintaining eye contact the entire time he fucked her mouth. She tried to alter his rhythm with licks and sucks. When he kept up the relentless pace, she slackened her jaw, her eyes closing as she relinquished control.

He held on for as long as he could, the sight of her lips on his dick feeding his hunger as much as the liquid heat. At the cusp of release, he pulled out, rock hard and ready to explode.

The carpet scraped Kim's breasts as Joss flipped her. Still burning from the balm he'd used, her nipples protested the abuse. But his rough handling fueled her arousal, which was already driven to a fever pitch by the aborted orgasm and blowjob.

She glanced up. To her relief, the other two Doms had left. Nonetheless, her face flamed. Strangers had stripped her naked, pinned her down, and watched her get wet from giving Joss oral.

No, she hadn't *given* him anything. He'd fucked her mouth, and she'd enjoyed every moment.

The scent of menthol assailed her moments before his large hands closed around her butt. She groaned as he smeared the cold, slippery liquid over flesh tender from a recent spanking. Within seconds, her ass heated, the icy-hot sting intensifying the soreness.

He'd used small quantities of the product on her before, the thick, clear compound serving as both lubricant and stimulant. Her labia were on fire. Her clit pulsed.

Hearing the crackle of tearing plastic, she twisted her head back. Her heart sank as she watched him pull out a butt plug. They'd never tried anal, and he seemed intent on making tonight one she'd never forget.

To her horror, he covered the conical plastic with ample amounts of the minty balm. As if he could read her mind, he answered her unvoiced question. "It'll help numb the pain. Trust me."

Curious enough not to stop him, she turned her face to the side. Cheek on the floor, she gritted her teeth as he pushed the plug into her. She closed her fingers over the carpet, her breaths devolving into gasps as the torture intensified. Tears torched the back of her lids. The safe word hovered on the tip of her tongue.

Then, with a plop, the agony ended, leaving

behind a steady, searing pressure.

"Good girl."

Taking her by the shoulders, he lifted her to her knees. Wedging himself between her calves, he brought her down until the tip of his penis touched her labia. At some point, he'd smoothed on a condom.

The crisp fabric of his trousers rasped her thighs. His chest warmed her back despite the shirt separating them. Plumping her breasts, he tugged at her swollen nipples. His rumbled words tickled the sensitive spot behind her ear. "This will hurt."

"Wait—"

He surged into her, the uncomfortable stretching overwhelmed by the impact of his groin hitting her ass. She cried out, her hips shimmying to escape the dual torture. With a whispered threat, he shifted his hands to circle her waist, his imprisoning grip forcing her to remain in place.

Left with no recourse, she stopped moving. Biting hard enough to mark her neck, he slid one hand down. His fingers settled on her clit. He pressed, circled, before spreading her labia and forcing direct contact.

White patches covered her vision. Her skin pulsed hot and cold. Stuffed beyond endurance, she slumped against his chest. Reaching her arms back, she used his broad shoulders as an anchor. "You're hurting me."

"You want me to."

She couldn't deny the simple truth. He lifted her up and down his thick length. Each time their bodies met, the plug shifted inside her, the edgy pain enhancing the pleasure of his assault. Combined with his wicked fingers, the chemical heat licking her breasts and butt, she stood no chance.

Ecstasy consumed her. Arching her spine, she circled her ass in a silent demand for more. Murmuring praises into her ear, he dug his fingers into her abs. He pulled her back to meet each thrust, his rhythm quickening until her teeth rattled and her breasts bounced.

Her awareness shattered, before coalescing into the narrowest of bands. Cognizant only of the man pounding into her, she screamed when the frustrating agony splintered. Spasming around his unrelenting impalement, she clung to him as he forced her to take him deeper, harder, and faster.

Chapter Six

"**A**re you sure you don't want to crash in my suite?" Joss nuzzled Kim's neck as they strode out the hotel's sliding glass doors. "My tub fits two. It has massaging jets."

The man had a knack for exploiting her weaknesses. A long soak sounded like heaven after the night's activities. Muscles she hadn't known existed protested each movement. With every step, her sore butt reminded her of the lines they'd crossed.

Thoroughly used, she was exhausted, giddy, and paradoxically hyper. A beautiful, sunny day beckoned. She'd trade it in a heartbeat for some indoor time with the Dom by her side.

Alas, she couldn't afford the distraction. Putting her life back on track came first. Coming clean to her employer, retrieving her original IDs, and digging up her ATM card topped her list of priorities. Then, she'd see about requesting an official university transcript, sprucing up her resume, and applying for a day job.

She'd keep her night one, perhaps shaving a few

hours here and there. It came with voyeuristic perks and extra cash.

Damn. She should call her parents and tell them everything. Maybe she could put that off until tomorrow.

As for Joss, she'd have to slot him into her suddenly hectic schedule. If he wanted to hang out, it meant sharing a one dollar Hot Pocket from her freezer and crashing on her lumpy mattress. The man better toughen up, and fast.

"You're the one who insisted I bring you home. Besides, I'm sure Tiger has destroyed your hotel room." She doubted the man realized cats had claws and needed litter.

Scowling, he adjusted the back of her top so it covered an extra quarter inch of her ribcage. A second later, the cotton rode up. He groaned. "Is there some reason you won't let me buy you a T-shirt?"

She wagged her finger. "Buying me stuff is against the rules." The new ones she'd instituted ever since it became clear they would one-night stand each other on a regular basis.

He wrapped his arms around her midriff. She suspected possessiveness drove him, not affection. Ever since they left the club, he'd gotten growly. "Rules are meant to be broken. Besides, I tore your shirt. It's not a gift. It's restitution."

Always the lawyer. "So, you can have your posse strip me, hold me down while I was naked, and watch me give you a blow job." She crossed her arms. "But showing off my abs outdoors rubs you the wrong way?"

"I can't be rational." He shrugged. "Not when

you're underdressed. We're not in a club. I don't trust dudes I haven't been friends with since kindergarten."

"It's Vegas. Since I have my pants back on, some would argue I'm overdressed. By the way, aren't you melting in that suit?"

Outside air-conditioned environs, just looking at his outfit made her overheat. At least he hadn't put on a tie.

"As a matter of fact.... Yes, I am." A triumphant gleam in his eyes, he shrugged off his jacket and deposited it on her shoulders.

Though the soft wool smelled enough like him to compel her to draw it closer, she narrowed her eyes. Outside a scene, she didn't want him getting any ideas about bossing her around. "Please tone down the caveman act. We've discussed this."

He stuck out his lower lip. "I'd lost you for close to a year. My memory needs refreshing. I have to warn you, all my teachers swear I'm a slow learner. Oh look, the damn car is rounding the corner." It'd taken them long enough. Considering Joss had called ahead, the vehicle's arrival should have been in sync with theirs.

"About time." She'd have to alert hotel management of the problem. When it came to classy, high-end experiences, the little details mattered.

"I'm considering not coughing up a tip." To her chagrin, Joss's mind seemed to move in lockstep with hers. "What kind of shitty outfit are you working for? You should quit and move back to Boston."

"Nice try." She scowled as the brand new convertible BMW inched closer. Despite a clear path, it moved at sub-turtle speed. What the heck? *That's* your car?'

"Don't worry. It's a rental. My new ride is a Ferrari. I switched from SUVs to sports cars."

"Isn't it a little soon for a midlife crisis?" she sputtered. "A Beemer won't survive ten minutes in my neighborhood. Couldn't you have picked something less ostentatious?"

"I have a minimum limit on horse power." He fluttered his lashes, the feigned innocence fooling no one. "Of course, we could drive this to my hotel, where it'll be safe."

Tempting. "Tiger will have peed on your mattress."

"We'll get another room."

"No, I refuse to let you spend any more money because of me." She exaggerated her sigh. "You leave me no choice. We're taking the bus."

He gaped. "The bus. As in public transportation?"

She fought back a grin. "Am I scaring you off, rich boy?"

"No. Of course not." For once, beads of sweat dotted his brow. "How about I switch the car for a Prius? The rental place is on the way, and I'll be *saving* money because of you."

Not a huge fan of the transit system, she relented. "Okay. Deal."

When the car reached them, Joss strode to the driver's side. She frowned. Ever since she'd spotted the valet through the front window, something about the nondescript man had smelled off. Trusting her instincts, she identified the source of her unease. The guy wore a long trench coat.

Uniform violations aside, the stifling heat made outerwear a rare sight in these parts. Even though the vehicle had come to a complete standstill, the driver lingered inside the cab, the delay long enough to prompt Joss to knock on the window.

The valet reached inside his coat. *Then*, he unlocked the car.

She didn't think. She acted.

Sprinting at full speed, she rammed the door as it swung open, crashing it into the exiting driver. With a loud wail, he tumbled onto the pavement. A hunk of black metal flew from his hand, landed on the ground, and skidded to a stop in front of Joss's lace-ups.

An M4, modded with a suppressor. What an amateur. Why bring a machine gun when a pistol would do the job?

Both men dove for the firearm. Though certain Joss had an advantage, she vaulted around the door to land a kick on the assassin's abdomen. Grunting, he rolled on his back, giving her the perfect opportunity to stomp on his balls.

Though cliché, the move worked like a charm.

In the meantime, Joss picked up the weapon and aimed it at their assailant's chest. Certain he had no idea how to use it, she picked her way to his side. "Want to give me that?"

"No." He sounded calm. Too calm.

She dug her fingers into his tensed forearm. The dumbass was down for the count. Though her heart continued to race, the danger ended moments ago. "Let's not start our relationship with a murder charge."

"I can argue a self-defense case in my sleep." He closed his hand around hers and tore it off. "He tried to kill you."

Oh God. The idiot might shoot. If he didn't brace the thing right, and assuming the assassin had modded it to full auto, bullets could spray all over the place.

Not good.

"Err…. Joss…. He wasn't aiming at me."

She watched his expression soften from one blink to the next. Having discovered the ideal strategy, she circled her arms around his waist and pressed her forehead into his lats. "I was on the other side of the door. If he'd wanted to kill me, he would have waited to grab the gun." The argument assumed the man wasn't an idiot, which recent events had brought into question.

Throwing a glance at the personnel in dark suits who'd run out of the hotel to form a semicircle around them, Joss lowered the weapon. "I guess bruised balls will do."

She drew in a deep breath. The man had warped priorities. He'd kill for her, but not himself. "Did you piss off any destitute mob bosses?" Considering the quality of their assassin, the bounty must have been pathetic.

"No. I do corporate law, with an occasional exception for friends." Against her cheek, his muscles remained tense. "There's no reason for anyone to kill me."

Although his personality tempted her to wring his neck every once in a while, she had to agree.

She tightened her hold on him. The timing couldn't be a coincidence. "What precisely did you do to get your mother off my back?"

He handed the firearm to one of the hotel's security staff. "All this PDA is great for my ego, but you can let me go. I can't move."

"You could have died." She hugged him closer. "I get to hold you as long as I want. What did you do, Joss?"

"I seized control of my trust fund and threatened to cut Mother off." He gave her shoulder an awkward pat. "Sandra hates poverty much more than she loves her sons. She's selfish that way. Besides, since I handed the FBI a case against my brother on a silver platter, your testimony is moot."

Her heart breaking for him, she tilted her head back. He was a smart guy. He hadn't reached the obvious conclusion because he didn't want to. For his own safety, they needed to face the truth. "What happens to the trust if you die?" She cupped his face, drew him down so she could brush her lips on his stubbled jaw.

His brows knotted. Then he threw his head back and laughed—it was one of the saddest sounds she'd ever heard. "Damn. I guess I left one giant, gaping loophole."

No son should have to anticipate his mother killing him for money. "I'm so sorry."

"For what?" He caught her chin then bit her lower lip. "Giving me sass in the club?"

Recognizing the diversion, she kissed him, pouring all the tenderness she had into the caress. As much as she understood his preference, she couldn't let him hide behind passion and games. "For breaking up your family. Joss...your mother tried to kill you. You can't ignore this."

"My family was broken long before we met." He ran his palms down her back, the movement slow and soothing. "Stop worrying. I'll handle it."

"How?"

He rolled his eyes. "You're nagging."

"This is the epitome of extenuating circumstances. Your life is at stake. Why won't you take this seriously?"

"I *am*. Fine. If you feel so strongly about my well-being, you won't mind marrying me."

At times, conversation with the man gave her headaches. "Come again?"

"If we're married, then you'll inherit everything when I die. Trust me, my mother will switch to sending me protein shakes."

"And if we both die?"

He scratched his chin. "Valid point. I'll stipulate in our will everything goes to charity if we don't have children."

"Can't you stipulate it without marrying me?"

"Okay. You got me there." He pouted. "Damn. Why does this trick work in TV shows?"

She smacked the side of his head. "Because it's a plot device. No, I'm not marrying you. I'm twenty-two."

"The average age of marriage for females in Utah is twenty-three point three."

The overconfident ass must have looked up the statistics before flying here. "And I'm from Mass. Come on, we need to find a lawyer and write your will. Who knows how many hired guns your mother sicced on you?"

"Pretty sure it's just the one. She spends a lot on drugs, and this is super-short notice. Even if she pawned her jewelry, she couldn't have come up with much." Joss pulled out his smartphone and started tapping. "I'll text her and say I'd already changed my will. I actually have. I did it eons ago. I forgot to tell her."

Text? The man was going to thwart a murder attempt via *text*? "Shouldn't you at least call?"

"The messaging app tells me when she's read it." He pocketed the gadget. "Which she has, as of two seconds ago. It'll take her five minutes to verify the terms with the lawyers and fix whatever she did."

"How do you know she'll do it quickly? Shouldn't you check—?"

"Don't worry, she'll haul ass. I left the entire Bradlee fortune to you, followed by your charity of choice, which I assumed was Green Peace."

"You did *what*?"

He patted her head. "I figured you'd put it to good use."

"Undo it. Undo it right now." With great difficulty, she kept her volume a few notches under a shriek. "Whether you're dead or alive, I don't want your money. If you didn't have all this gold-plated baggage, we wouldn't be in this mess."

"I knew there was a reason I loved you." He hooked his arm around her elbow and dragged her toward the car. "Come on. Let's get out of here before the cops show up. I have better things to do with my day than signing stupid statements. By the way, are you hungry? I'm starved."

About the Author

Globetrotter, lover of languages, and romance author, Tara Quan has an addiction for crafting tales with a pinch of spice and a smidgen of kink. Inspired by her travels, Tara enjoys tossing her kick-ass heroines and alpha males into exotic contemporary locales, paranormal worlds, and post-apocalyptic futures. Her characters, armed with magical powers or conventional weapons, are guaranteed a suspenseful and sensual ride, as well as their own happily ever after. To receive updates about her new releases and get a free sexy read, subscribe to her mailing list at

www.taraquan.com/newsletter.

Also by Tara Quan